"Didn't you see the sign?" Conrad roared

"I wasn't looking for signs," Marnie said in a croaking voice. "I was looking at the water."

His hands reached out to grab her shoulders, shaking her. "Do you realize how close you came to drowning?" he rasped angrily. "If I hadn't spotted you when I did, you would be dead!"

Tears sprang to Marnie's eyes. "Yes, I know. Th-thanks for saving me." She was shivering with shock and reaction.

The anger seemed to leave him as suddenly as it came. And then he cradled her in his arms, holding her gently, warming her, reassuring her. "Let's get you home," he whispered against her ear.

Marnie marveled how nicely she seemed to fit under his arm, as though he'd been made just for her. *Stop it*, she scolded herself. *You're pretending again. This man is Helena's!*

Books by Rosemary Badger

HARLEQUIN ROMANCE

2617—CORPORATE LADY
2629—A GIRL CALLED ANDY
2695—A TIME OF DECEPTION
2749—A MATTER OF MARNIE

These books may be available at your local bookseller.

Don't miss any of our special offers. Write to us at the following address for information on our newest releases.

Harlequin Reader Service
P.O. Box 52040, Phoenix, AZ 85072-2040
Canadian address: P.O. Box 2800, Postal Station A,
5170 Yonge St., Willowdale, Ont. M2N 6J3

A Matter of Marnie

Rosemary Badger

Harlequin Books

TORONTO • NEW YORK • LONDON
AMSTERDAM • PARIS • SYDNEY • HAMBURG
STOCKHOLM • ATHENS • TOKYO • MILAN

Original hardcover edition published in 1985
by Mills & Boon Limited

ISBN 0-373-02749-4

Harlequin Romance first edition March 1986

This is for Lee

———————————————————————————

Printed in U.S.A.

CHAPTER ONE

'YOU'RE saying my grandmother is a *thief*?' The man sitting behind the desk choked the words. His face was black with anger and Marnie stared at him, her violet coloured eyes large with dismay.

'I'm not saying anything of the kind,' she denied, her voice soft and reassuring. She swallowed hard. 'Your grandmother has been in the shop a few times and quite often she forgets to pay for the items she buys.'

'Forgets to pay?' Conrad Wright rose slowly from his chair and glared down at the petite young woman sitting demurely in her chair. 'Doesn't "forgets to pay" mean she has been shoplifting?'

'No, I'm sure in her case it's a genuine case of forgetfulness. She gets flustered,' Marnie went on to explain. 'Her Christmas list worries her and . . .'

Conrad Wright ripped a wallet out of his hip pocket and threw several large bills across his desk. 'Whatever my grandmother has *forgotten* to pay for, I'm sure this should settle the account,' he rasped angrily.

Marnie didn't look at the money. Her eyes were on Conrad Wright. 'I'm afraid you have misunderstood me, Mr Wright,' she said. 'I'm not here to cause trouble for your grandmother. We know her address and we merely send the accounts to her. It's just that I've become terribly fond of her and I can't help feeling sorry for her.'

'Sorry for my grandmother?' he asked incredulously. 'Do you happen to know who *she* is . . .? Who *we* are?'

A smile appeared on Marnie's lips. 'Of course I know who you are,' she said, almost indulgently. 'One would have to be blind not to see all the billboards displaying your name. In fact,' she replied, her eyes wandering to the glass panelled wall overlooking Castlereagh Street, which ran through the heart of Sydney's downtown district, 'I see your construction group is building the new underground shopping complex across the street.'

'That's right,' he growled meaningfully, 'so you can see your sympathies are wasted on my grandmother. She doesn't want for a thing.'

'Maybe not material things,' Marnie was willing to agree. 'But she certainly lacks companionship.'

'Companionship!?' Conrad Wright scoffed at the word. 'When you get to be my grandmother's age you don't need companionship.'

Marnie shook her head. 'You're quite wrong, Mr Wright. I believe your grandmother is in desperate need of company. Have you ever considered employing a companion for her? Someone she could chat with, shop with, discuss grandchildren and, well, even the weather?'

The tall, athletic looking man glared down at her, his darkly handsome features regarding her with a large measure of suspicion.

'Ah,' he said. 'So that's why you have come.' His black eyes roamed her face, a humourless smile twisting the hard line of his mouth. Marnie watched him, her large violet eyes guileless in the small oval of her face.

'Yes,' she said, relieved that she had at last been able to get through to this tough, arrogant man. 'Sometimes it takes an outsider to see things the way they truly are.' She rose to her feet, a small figure dressed in a simple white frock, her short black hair curving femininely around her cheeks. 'I have the name of an agency here,' she said, opening her handbag and getting out a small white card. 'I've taken the liberty to speak to them myself and they have assured me that all their applicants are thoroughly screened and come with the highest of references.' Marnie held the card out to him. 'If you just telephone they will send someone around for you and your grandmother to interview right away.'

He stared at the proffered card. 'You mean you aren't volunteering for the job yourself?'

'Oh, no.' And then seeing the expression on his face, smiled. 'As much as I like your grandmother,' she said softly, 'I hardly qualify as a companion.'

He took the card and without sparing it a glance placed it on the smooth polished top of his desk. 'I'm a busy man, Miss Hamilton,' he drawled, and Marnie noticed it was the first time since she had made an appointment to see him and had introduced herself that he had called her by her name. 'I don't have time to interview companions.'

A small frown creased the smooth line of her brow and then her expression cleared. 'Would you like me to do it?' she asked helpfully. 'I think I know just the type of person your grandmother would enjoy having as her companion.'

When he didn't answer Marnie continued in that same helpful tone: 'I could interview two or three. Your grandmother could sit in on the interviews and when she has decided which one she would like you can have a talk with them both.'

When he still didn't contribute anything, Marnie wet her lips and continued a little breathlessly. 'The only thing left for you to do would be to determine a wage and ... and the hours.' She looked up at him appealingly. 'How does that sound?'

He shoved his hands into his pockets and exhaled sharply. 'How well do you know my grandmother?' he asked, dismissing her question with one of his own.

'Well, as I've already told you, she's been in the shop several times and twice we've had lunch together when

she had finished her shopping and it was time for my
lunch break.' Marnie suddenly felt very unsure of
herself, not liking the way Mr Wright was regarding her
through narrowed eyes. 'It just sort of happened that
way,' she offered, feeling somehow that it was necessary
to offer some sort of explanation of how she came to be
lunching with his grandmother.

Conrad Wright nodded absently and then sat back
down at his desk. He picked up a gold pen and twisted
it around in his large tanned hands. Marnie remained
standing, wondering as she watched him if he had
forgotten she was still in his office.

Presently he laid the pen aside and leaned back in
his chair, regarding her through hooded eyes. 'A
companion for my grandmother might not be such a
bad idea,' he said slowly, as though still trying hard
to get used to the fact. 'With Christmas coming up
and with the house usually filled with guests, she
tends to get in the way.' He raised his arms and
folded his hands behind his head. 'How would you
like the job?'

'I've already told you . . .'

'I know what you've told me,' he cut in impatiently.
'You said you weren't qualified as a companion. But I
say you are. Besides you already know my grandmother
and obviously you care for her if you've taken all this
trouble to see to her welfare.'

'But I've already got a job, Mr Wright. Besides, I'm
not after permanent employment. I'm only working
during the holidays until school starts again. You see
I'm a teacher and I help my aunt out in her shop during
school holidays.'

His black eyes trailed over her slender figure, coming
to rest on her face. 'You hardly look like a teacher,' he
said, a brief smile touching his lips and lighting up his
dark features. 'More like a student.' His smile

broadened. 'But I should imagine you've heard that put to you many times before.'

Marnie didn't return his smile. 'I think you are deliberately trying to flatter me, Mr Wright,' she said evenly, 'in order to persuade me into becoming your grandmother's companion.'

He shrugged broad shoulders and laughed. 'Whatever it will take, Miss Hamilton.' His eyes glittered with amusement.

'I accept the position,' she told him quietly, her large violet eyes meeting his dark ones squarely.

His eyes widened in surprise, but she noted how he quickly masked his expression. 'What made you decide?'

'You did.'

He shot her an enquiring glance. 'So you are open to flattery just as I suspected.' His voice was smug.

'I hardly consider your comment about looking more like a student than a teacher as a form of flattery, Mr Wright. No, it was one other comment you made which decided me. It was when you said your grandmother tends to get in your way. I think I decided then that I would like to be her companion.'

His unusually dark skin fused with anger. 'And what about your aunt, Miss Hamilton? Casting her needs aside so you can help a stranger instead?'

Marnie drew herself up to her full height which wasn't much over five feet five inches. 'My aunt doesn't really need me in the shop. She has my two cousins to help her.'

'So,' he drawled, 'like my grandmother you would only be in the way?'

'If it makes you happy to think so, then, yes you're probably right.'

He regarded her in silence for several seconds before finally asking: 'When can you start?'

'How about Monday?'

'Why not tomorrow?'

'Tomorrow is Saturday.'

'And you only want to work five days a week. Right?'

'Well, it is customary,' she replied a little huffily, wondering why she was allowing this man to get under her skin.

'Monday to Friday, nine to five?' he asked sarcastically.

'Well, yes, I suppose so.'

'I'm sorry, but that won't do. Do you live with your aunt?'

'No, of course not. I have my own flat in Paddington.'

His black brows shot up. 'That's a trendy district,' he said meaningfully.

Hot colour seared Marnie's cheeks. 'I happen to teach in Paddington,' she issued stiffly.

He got up and walked over to the glass-panelled wall, staring down at the busy street below. 'If my grandmother needs a companion then I think she should have one on a twenty-four basis.' He swung around to look at her. 'For the duration of your school holidays I want you to move into my house where you can spend all your time with her.'

Marnie stared at him, speechless. She could hardly believe her ears. Then with difficulty she managed to find her voice. 'I'm not used to being ordered around, Mr Wright,' she said stiffly. 'And I doubt if your grandmother needs round-the-clock supervision.'

A muscle twitched alongside his jaw as he held himself rigid, apparently amazed that anyone should question or contradict his commands. 'May I remind you, Miss Hamilton, that you came to me with this proposition.'

'It wasn't a proposition, Mr Wright, it was merely a suggestion for the good of your grandmother. I've accepted the position but I have no intention of moving into your house.' Where you are, she felt like adding.

He crossed the room and stood beside his desk only inches from where Marnie was still standing. His closeness had an alarming effect on her senses and it was with great difficulty that she managed to keep her gaze from faltering before the fierce blackness of his penetrating probe.

'You mentioned that you sent my grandmother's accounts to my house.'

Marnie nodded, not trusting herself to speak with a throat which had gone suddenly dry.

'Then you must realise that our house is a fair distance from Paddington.'

Marnie lowered her eyes. She hadn't thought about the distance which separated the two places of residence. The Wright estate was some forty kilometres up the coast and by the time she fought the downtown traffic the trip each way would take well over an hour, possibly even two. The prospect of travelling close to eighty kilometres a day in her little car wasn't at all inviting.

'If you can manage the trip each day then I guess I can, too,' she said, her eyes sweeping up to his face.

'But I don't manage the trip each day,' he returned softly, a hint of humour threading through his voice. 'I usually camp at construction sites and when it's necessary for me to spend a few days at the office, then I stay at my town house.'

Marnie tore her eyes away from his mocking face, wishing she had heeded her aunt's advice not to get involved with poor Mrs Wright, as they had all come to call her due to her friendless state.

'I'll tell you what,' he went on, leaning his chin in his

hand as though deep in thought, 'come out to the house on Monday prepared to spend the week. If you find us too inhospitable then you can leave at the end of the week. Either I'll forget the whole idea of a companion for my grandmother or I'll find someone else to take your place.'

'Well, all right,' Marnie agreed reluctantly, a tentative smile forming on her lips. 'Tell your grandmother to expect me Monday morning around ten.'

'Good.' He held out his hand and Marnie extended her own and he took it and held it and Marnie felt a thrill of apprehension sweep through her body. She pulled her hand away and placed it firmly on the strap of her shoulder bag, turning towards the door as she did so. His large hand snaked out and wrapped itself around the doorknob.

'I'll be looking forward to seeing you Monday,' he drawled, peering down at her from his towering height.

'I'll be looking forward to seeing your *grandmother*,' Marnie returned pointedly.

His soft chuckle followed her all the way down to her car parked outside in the street. When she sat down for dinner at her aunt and uncle's place later that evening she could still hear that soft taunting sound in the back of her head.

'I had a letter from Mum and Dad,' Marnie told her aunt and uncle and two cousins. 'They're still in Africa and looking forward to their first safari. They're having the time of their lives.'

'I received one too,' her aunt told her. 'But there was no mention when they would be home.'

'Oh, they won't be back for ages yet,' Marnie laughed, helping herself to the roast potatoes her cousin passed her. 'Dad and Mum have planned this trip for years and after Africa they sail on to Europe.'

Dessert was almost over before her aunt remembered about Marnie's appointment with Conrad Wright, and questioned her about it.

At the mention of his name Marnie felt her heartbeat quicken and hot colour flooded her cheeks. With her parents away her aunt and uncle felt duty bound to invite her for dinner each Friday evening so she knew there would be no escaping telling them about her meeting with Mr Wright and what had resulted from it.

Her aunt regarded her with dismay. 'You mean you agreed to becoming his grandmother's companion?'

Marnie treated the matter as casually as she could. 'I'm on a week's trial,' she told the interested faces around the table. 'If it doesn't work out then at least I've had a holiday on the coast.'

'I don't like it,' her uncle put in sternly. 'Young Wright has a reputation with the ladies. I don't think your father would approve of you spending a day, never mind a week, in his company.'

Marnie laughed softly and looked affectionately across at her uncle, her father's brother. 'I'm quite capable of looking after myself,' she told him fondly, adding reassuringly, 'I doubt I'll be having much to do with Mr Wright. It's his grandmother I'll be spending my time with.'

'Just the same,' her uncle went on, 'you'll be alone in that house with him and . . .'

'Dad, for goodness sake!' chimed in her plump cousin. 'Marnie is twenty-three years old and Mr Wright must be at least thirty-two if he's a day. They're not kids!'

'Gosh, but he's handsome!' added Marnie's second cousin, who was plump like her sister and their mother. 'He's forever in the social pages.' Her eyes looked enviously at Marnie's pretty face and slender figure. 'I wish it was me going out to his place.'

'That will be enough,' her father put in sternly and then looked across at his niece. 'You're quite sure you want to take this job?'

Marnie nodded. 'It might only be for a week,' she reminded him, 'but if everything works out it still will only be for the holidays. Besides, his grandmother certainly needs somebody.'

'That she does,' her aunt agreed with an emphatic shake of her head. 'I don't think that woman is eating properly. She's been a customer of ours for years but I got a real shock when I saw her in the shop with her Christmas list. She's down to skin and bones!'

Marnie spent the weekend cleaning her flat, defrosting the refrigerator and washing and ironing the clothes she planned to take with her for her week's stay at Conrad Wright's residence.

She left early Monday morning hoping to beat the commuter traffic as people made their way from the northern coastal suburbs down to their city jobs. Traffic thinned out after Manly and by the time she drove through Narrabeen, following the coast up past Avalon to Palm Beach, hers was practically the only car on the road heading north. The morning sun was soft and pleasant and the salt air was refreshing coming off the sparkling blue waters of the Pacific Ocean.

Rocky cliffs gave way to white sandy beaches and quite often she slowed down to watch a surfer ride his board on huge rolling waves. A thrill of excitement encompassed her as she wondered if the Wright estate was overlooking the beach or if it was tucked away somewhere in a wooded glen. Either way it would be good to be away from the city for a while and breathe in wholesome country air.

Her aunt had been able to give her a general description of where the property was located and she knew she was in the vicinity now, having passed the last coastal home.

The empty road stretched out in front of her with bush on one side, ocean on the other. She hadn't realised the estate would be so hidden and she began to fear perhaps she had passed the sign indicating the Wright property. Just as she was about to swing the car around and retrace the last few miles, a neat but rather small sign bore the name she was looking for.

Marnie swung the car into the drive which was on the ocean front. The driveway was lined with graceful Alexander Palm trees, their shining fronds swaying in the early morning sea breezes. The driveway seemed to go on forever and it wasn't until Marnie rounded a curve that the house loomed up in front of her.

It was huge! Flanked by green sweeping lawns, flower gardens and native shrubs, it rose majestically into the blue cloudless sky. Made of sandstone brick it was early colonial in design with bottom and top verandahs supported by gleaming white pillars. The windows were long and narrow with white shutters and she guessed that they all opened on to the verandahs like doors.

She drove slowly up the paved drive, bringing her car to a stop in front of the wide steps leading up to the massive oak door. A gleaming brass knocker sat in the centre of the door and she guessed something as huge as that was definitely needed if anyone was to hear if a visitor had arrived.

Marnie got out of the car, dragging her suitcase after her. A gardener peeped up from a row of shrubs he had been weeding beside the steps, and looked at her curiously, but then went back to his work without saying a word and Marnie wondered with reddened cheeks if he was quite used to seeing young ladies arriving at the mansion with a suitcase in their hands!

She lifted the brass knocker several times before the door was finally opened by a large, raw-boned housekeeper of middle age. The housekeeper wore a white uniform and had a large apron tied around her ample waist. Her face was cheerless and her grey hair was swept back into a tight bun. She regarded Marnie through cold, faded blue eyes for several seconds before recognition dawned.

'Well!' she exclaimed. 'You must be the young lady Mr Wright was telling me about.'

Marnie smiled, relieved that she wouldn't have to offer any explanations of why she was here.

'Yes, I'm Marnie Hamilton,' she said softly.

The housekeeper swung the door open wider and a thin sneer appeared on her lips. 'Come in,' she said, stepping aside as Marnie crossed the threshold. 'I don't see why Mr Wright has suddenly decided to get someone to take care of old Mrs Wright.' Her faded eyes swept over Marnie's slender form and she shook her head as though not quite believing that anyone of Marnie's stature could possibly do the job. 'I'm Mrs Thompson,' she said, introducing herself, 'but just call me Flora. I'm the housekeeper and with only Annie to help me I suppose it is too much taking care of this place plus old Mrs Wright as well. Just wait here a minute and I'll fetch Annie to show you to your room.' And with that she was gone and Marnie was left to mull over what Flora had told her and to take in her surroundings. She was in a large vestibule or entrance hall with dark panelled walls and a black-and-white tiled floor. She couldn't help but notice that the tiles were badly in need of a good washing and waxing and that the several pieces of period furniture were thick with dust. Across from where she stood, sliding glass doors were opened to reveal a sun room.

Marnie crossed over to look at the room. It was large and bright and airless. She fought the temptation to open the french doors which led on to the wide patio and which would have let in the sea breezes. From where she stood she could see the ocean through the breaks in the trees. The furniture in the room was comfortable looking and covered in a floral print material of greens and blues and beiges. The soft green carpeting looked as if it hadn't been vacuumed for a long time nor, she saw with a wry grimace, had any of the furniture been dusted for the same length of time. With a bit of sprucing up the room would have been extremely inviting and Marnie had the feeling that once it had been.

A noise made her turn around. A young girl of about eighteen was standing watching her, holding her suitcase. 'I'm Annie,' she supplied sullenly, 'Flora says I'm to show you to your room.'

'Thank you, Annie,' Marnie murmured with a smile. 'But there's no need for you to carry my suitcase,' she said, reaching for it, only to have Annie swing it out of her reach.

As Marnie followed the reluctant Annie through a long, wide corridor and up a curving staircase she couldn't help but notice the general air of neglect which seemed to be everywhere. The furnishings were mostly priceless antiques but the beauty of their carvings was hidden under thick layers of dust. Several times she sneezed as she breathed in the tiny molecules, and she couldn't help but wonder what the state of her room would be in if this was a fair example of Flora's housekeeping.

The room Annie showed her filled her with delight and expelled any fears that she might have to embarrass the housekeeper by asking for a vacuum cleaner and several large dusters! The room was huge and spotless. A large canopied bed had pride of place in the centre of the floor and the pink spread matched the pink velvet curtains covering the windows. The french doors leading on to the verandah were open and a cool sea breeze filled the air. On one side of the room there was a two-seater couch and an armchair, the floral print of small pink orchids matching in colour the bedspread and curtains. Thick beige carpeting covered the floor and the whole room had a feeling of spaciousness and luxury and deep comfort.

'Why, this is beautiful!' Marnie exclaimed with enthusiasm.

Annie was pleased and the look of sullenness was replaced with a look of gratitude. 'I did it out myself,' she confided. 'Mr Wright said you were to have this room and it took the whole weekend getting it ready. Your bathroom is through that door,' she pointed with a stubby finger, 'and old Mrs Wright's room is down the hall just next to this one.'

'Where is Mrs Wright now?' Marnie asked as she started to open her suitcase. She looked up at Annie. 'It's such a lovely day I suppose she's out wandering somewhere through the gardens.'

Annie shook her head, a surprised look on her face. 'Oh, no, Miss Hamilton,' she said. 'Old Mrs Wright never goes out of her room unless it's necessary. The stairs are too much for her and we can't always be around to help her up and down. She mostly stays in her room.'

Marnie straightened from her unpacking. 'Stays in her room?' she asked incredulously. 'You mean that's where she is right this minute?'

'Of course! Flora said not to tell her you had arrived until after you've had a chance to settle yourself in. Flora said she would only get in your way. Anyway, she's probably napping. That's all she ever seems to do.' Annie looked down at the clothes Marnie had put out on the bed. 'Do you want me to put those away for you?' she asked, obviously considering Marnie's wardrobe to be far more interesting than discussing old Mrs Wright.

'No thank you, Annie. I can manage by myself now,' she answered quietly, but politely dismissing the girl.

Annie shrugged and walked towards the door. 'Will you be coming downstairs for lunch?' she asked.

'I'll see what Mrs Wright wants to do,' Marnie informed her, and then, 'Where is Mr Wright? Is he home?'

'No, we haven't seen him since Friday evening but he said he would be back tonight.'

'Good!' Marnie exclaimed. 'As soon as he comes in will you let me know?'

'It might be late.'

'That's all right. I don't mind how late it is.'

After Annie had gone Marnie laid down the dress she was holding and stepped out into the hall, looking at the closed door Annie had indicated would be Mrs Wright's bedroom. There were no sounds coming from behind the door but surely Mrs Wright wouldn't be napping so early in the day? Marnie checked her watch. It was barely ten-thirty. She knocked softly on the door. When there was no response she twisted the knob and opened the door. The room was in almost total darkness and the air was hot and stuffy. Marnie stepped inside and was barely able to make out the frail form of Mrs Wright sitting quietly in a chair. Marnie crossed the room towards her.

'Mrs Wright?' she asked softly. 'Are you awake?'

'Is that you, Annie?' Mrs Wright whispered in a tiny voice. 'Has my grandson come back yet?' She blinked up at Marnie, not recognising her in the dark gloom of the room.

Marnie touched her gently on the shoulder and leaned towards her. 'It's Marnie Hamilton, Mrs Wright,' she said. 'We've had lunch together and . . .'

Mrs Wright grasped her hand. 'You've come! Conrad said you would but I didn't dare hope . . . a young girl

like you ... why would you want to be ... what was it
Conrad said ...? Oh yes, now I remember ... a
companion, wasn't it?'

Marnie smiled down at her. 'Yes, that's right,' she
agreed gently. 'And I've been looking forward to it.'
She looked across at the shuttered windows. 'Were you
napping?'

Mrs Wright was surprised by the question. 'Oh no,'
she said. 'Sometimes I have a wee nap after lunch but
mostly I just sit and think.'

'Would you mind if I drew the curtains and opened
some windows? It's terribly hot in here.'

'Is it? I hadn't noticed, but yes, please do whatever
you wish.'

Marnie drew the curtains and opened the french door
leading on to the verandah. Immediately fresh fragrant
air sifted through the room, effectively dismissing the
staleness and the gloom.

Marnie was appalled by Mrs Wright's appearance. In
the shop she had been well dressed and nicely groomed.
But now her face seemed older and haggard and her
hair hadn't been combed from her night's sleep and she
was still in her bathrobe. Her bed hadn't been made
and the furniture was heavy with dust. Anger welled in
Marnie's throat and left a bitter taste in her mouth.

'Does your grandson ever visit you in your room?'
she asked, striving hard to keep her anger out of her
voice.

'Good heavens, no! Why would Conrad ever come in
here?'

To check on things, Marnie fumed, but wisely held
her tongue. The bedroom was a disgrace and it was
obvious poor Mrs Wright was being terribly and sadly
neglected. The odour of burnt toast came to her nostrils
and it was then that Marnie noticed the remains of
what might have been called a breakfast. She picked up

a plate and looked at the burnt toast which had a few nibbles taken from it.

'Did Flora cook you this?' she asked incredulously.

'Oh my, no,' Mrs Wright answered. 'I always make my own breakfast and lunch. Poor Flora is too busy with such a large house to look after and Annie, bless her heart, isn't much help.'

Marnie put the plate down and wandered over to an alcove. The alcove contained everything which a well-equipped kitchen might, right down to a microwave oven.

'Conrad had all this installed for me,' Mrs Wright said with pride and affection. 'He's away a lot and he knows how I hate eating my meals alone in the dining room and it's so much cosier and easier for me to fix something for myself up here. That way I eat what I want when I want and I'm no trouble to anyone.'

Marnie turned to face her and she was overwhelmed by the sadness and loneliness which was in the old lady's eyes and in the rejected slump of her shoulders.

'Who shops for you?' Marnie asked then.

Mrs Wright shrugged. 'Flora or Annie. Annie comes up and stocks the fridge and the cupboard once a week.'

Marnie opened the small fridge. There was some butter, a half a loaf of bread and some hard looking cheese. In the cupboard there was a large box of biscuits, some tea bags, a bowl of sugar and two cans of tomato soup. A cockroach scurried across the shelf and crawled up the open sugar bowl. Marnie shut the door and leaned against it.

'I'm really very happy that I have come here, Mrs Wright,' she said softly, 'because I intend making a great many changes to your life!'

CHAPTER TWO

'YOU'VE only been here twelve hours and already you've upset the entire household!' roared Conrad.

It's about time somebody upset things around here!' Marnie lashed back, her voice quivering with barely concealed fury.

Conrad glared down at her. 'Do you realise Christmas isn't far away and Flora and Annie are both threatening to quit their jobs?'

'Had it been up to me I wouldn't have given them a chance to quit! I would have fired them ages ago!'

'Did you have to accuse them of neglecting my grandmother? Did you have to order her room to be fumigated? The whole upstairs stinks and I have guests coming. I must have been mad to hire you.'

Marnie sat down in a chair. Her violet coloured eyes were almost black from exhaustion. Conrad had come home over an hour ago to be met by Flora and Annie who were threatening to hand in their resignations. Marnie had hoped to get to him first but the two women had beaten her to it and painted their own pictures, making Marnie out to be the villain. Conrad had sent for her in his study and she had expected anger but not cold-blooded rage. In her tired state she had responded with an anger which matched his and which had been quietly simmering the whole day as more and more events unfolded which pointed out to the cruel neglect of a very old lady.

'You've given me a week's trial,' Marnie said now in a quiet voice. 'If you will let me I would like to stay for the whole summer.'

Conrad sat down wearily on a chair across from her. He looked tired and, judging from his clothes, a pair of jeans and a plaid shirt, it was obvious he had been inspecting one of his building sites. His grandmother had mentioned several times during the day just how hard he worked maintaining and expanding the family business, which had been allowed to run down during the regime of his father who preferred gambling and women to work. He ran his hands through the thick black mass of his hair, and Marnie felt sorry for both him and his grandmother with no one reliable to look after them. But any softening she may have felt in regards to him was quickly dispelled when he raised his face and she saw his anger hadn't subsided.

'I can't afford to keep you,' he said coldly.

Marnie's eyes widened in surprise. 'How do you mean? Surely money can't be the problem ...'

'Of course it's not the money,' he snarled impatiently. He jumped up from his chair and shoved his hands into his jeans pockets. 'The only person you haven't upset is the gardener but then I hear you didn't go out much today. I can't afford to keep someone on my staff who's obviously bent on causing trouble.' He turned away from her and stared out the darkened window. 'Flora and Annie say they will quit unless I get rid of you.'

'So let them quit. They're not doing their jobs.'

He swung back to her, his black eyes smouldering with contempt. 'Are you crazy?' he rasped. 'I depend on them. Who do you suppose looks after my grandmother when I'm not here? Short of putting her in a Home, there's nothing I can do except hold on to those two and hope through conscience if nothing else they will do their best for Grandmother.'

'It seems to me none of you have done your best. When was the last time you inspected your grand-mother's room? Oh sure,' she raced on when he started to protest, 'you built that little kitchen for her and with Flora and Annie at the helm, they've virtually made her a prisoner right under your nose. Talk about burying your head in the sand!'

'That kitchen was put in at Grandmother's request. She has everything at her fingertips. She can make herself a cup of tea without having to bother anyone to do it for her.'

'Bother anyone? That's just it. You've all made her feel she's nothing but a nuisance!'

'Don't be ridiculous!' he snarled.

'But you have all said it. When I first met you in your office you said your grandmother gets in the way. Flora hinted the same thing only seconds after my arrival and Annie said it when she showed me to my room. You've all managed to convince yourselves that your grandmother is a nuisance and have conveyed the message loud and clear to the dear old soul.'

His face was black with anger and there was disbelief in his eyes. Marnie met his gaze without flinching. If she was to help his grandmother then she must convince him that his grandmother needed that help.

'What are you after?' he asked harshly. 'What was the real purpose of coming to my office on Friday?'

Marnie sighed. 'I thought I had explained all that,' she offered simply.

'You said my grandmother needed a companion. I agreed to it thinking you would take her on outings. I come home and find you've stirred up a hornet's nest. Now I'm asking you why?'

Marnie ran her hands along the arm rests of the leather chair she was sitting on. 'The hornet's nest was already here,' she returned stoutly. 'Somebody had to stir it up sooner or later.' Her eyes swept up to his face and she saw the tired lines etched around his mouth and eyes and for some unaccountable reason she had an almost overwhelming desire to smooth those lines away. She took a deep breath, conscious that her heart was beating a wild tattoo in her chest.

'Listen, Conrad,' she said softly, her voice gentle. 'My aunt has known your grandmother for a long time. She couldn't get over the change in her when she came into the shop to do her Christmas shopping. Your grandmother seemed so lost and lonely and she seemed incapable of keeping her thoughts straight. That comes from spending too much time alone. She needs to be stimulated, looked after, and above all she needs to feel loved. You put that kitchen in for her thinking she was having a great time cooking for herself and I know you thought she was eating properly.' Marnie took a deep breath, very much aware that he was watching her intently. 'Your grandmother has been existing on soup and biscuits for months now.'

'I wondered how long it would take before you brought that up,' he said almost jeeringly. Then at the astonished look on Marnie's face continued gratingly: 'Didn't you think Flora and Annie would have something to offer in their own defence? A hot meal is always served to my grandmother in the evenings. Tonight it was roast chicken and vegetables which you returned to the kitchen saying it was unsuitable for human consumption!'

'And it was!' Marnie flashed back, her patience deserting her. 'God knows how long that chicken must have been sitting in the fridge because it certainly had an unsavoury odour attached to it! And the vegetables were leftovers from some other meal and they had been fried into black crisps,' she declared hotly.

'I don't believe you,' he answered bluntly. 'The meal was good enough for Flora and Annie. They don't profess to be Cordon Bleu chefs.'

Marnie sighed in exasperation. 'The meal didn't have

to be good enough for Flora and Annie. They weren't the ones who had to eat it. When I took our plates down to the kitchen, they were eating a cheese omelette. I prepared an omelette for your grandmother and myself and we ate it in the upstairs den.'

'I'll question my grandmother in the morning,' he said coldly and then without warning pulled Marnie out of the chair. 'If you're lying about any of this so help me God I'll thrash you!'

Marnie glared up at him, resenting his superior height. 'I'm not lying!'

A strange light gleamed in his eyes and his hands tightened on her shoulders and she could feel his touch burning through the thin fabric of her blouse. 'Then you have nothing to worry about.'

He released her and she felt suddenly cold. She shivered, a gesture he was quick to notice and equally quick to misinterpret. A knowing smile crossed his lips. 'Shaking in your boots?'

Marnie backed away from him, hating him. She turned towards the door, walking quickly towards it.

'Where have you got my grandmother bedded down for the night?' he stopped her by asking. Marnie swung round to face him, her expression puzzled.

'She's in her room of course. Where else would she be?'

His black eyes kindled with a new light. 'In her room?' he exploded, the light in his eyes bursting into flame. 'But you've had the upstairs fumigated! She will be sickened by the fumes!'

Marnie felt a wild surge of hysteria rising in her throat. Frantically she tried to stifle it. She had been under a strain the whole day and her nerve ends were raw. The sight of Conrad's face with its ferocious glare had been too much. She felt like crying and she couldn't speak.

'I think you had better answer me, Miss Hamilton,' Conrad rounded on her harshly.

'I'm sorry,' Marnie gasped, wiping away a tear. 'I wasn't avoiding the question, truly I wasn't. It's just that I don't think I've ever spent a day quite like this one and when I saw the expression on your face when you were saying about the upstairs being fumigated, well . . .'

'Well, what?' he snapped.

'The upstairs *hasn't* been fumigated. We merely sprayed the room with a pesticide and put some 'roach traps in the cupboard. That's what you smelt when you went upstairs, but it's quite safe I can assure you.'

'So,' he ground out, sweeping a large hand through his hair. 'Why didn't you tell me before? Why have me think the upstairs bedrooms would be out of bounds for the next few days?'

'You didn't give me a chance to explain earlier. You were too busy accusing me of all sorts of things to listen to anything I had to say.' She turned again towards the door. 'What time do you wish to discuss matters with your grandmother?' she asked, pausing at the opened door.

'After breakfast.'

Marnie woke early the next morning, The sun was streaming into her room. The bedside clock told her it was only five-thirty. She tossed her covers aside and swung her long legs out of bed, stretching and yawning as she padded barefoot over to the french doors leading on to the balcony. Standing on the balcony she breathed in the clean salt air and her eyes rested on the swimming pool almost directly below. *Chaise-longues* and yellow umbrellas were grouped around the poolside. Large white stands were dotted intermittently around the pool, shining green ferns flowing from their sides.

Her eyes wandered from the scene below to the strip of green water which reached out from clean white sands. The pounding of the surf beckoned to her and with a smile on her lips she turned back to her bedroom and within minutes she was dressed in a bright red bikini. Grabbing a towel from her bathroom, she let herself out of her room and after first checking to make sure Mrs Wright was still sleeping soundly, raced down the long corridor, down the stairs and out one of the french doors, winging her way across the landscaped gardens to the beach beyond.

The soft sand felt warm under her bare feet. She walked to the water's edge and tested the foamy surf with a hesitant toe. It wasn't as cold as she had thought it might be so early in the morning. She spread her towel on the sand and then raced into the water, jack-knifing into the rolling green waves. Surfacing, she shook the water from her head and pushed her shining black cap of hair behind her ears. She could see Conrad's house from here, the sandstone brick appearing pink in the early morning sun. Palm trees stood erect in the still air, their leafy green fronds a pretty contrast against the pink brick. Sprawling frangipani trees with deep reds, soft pinks and creamy white blossoms blended in with the palms, and she could see the dark green hibiscus shrubs with their golden blooms nestled against the side of the house.

Marnie turned away from this splendour and rolled on to her back, the salty swell of the waves holding her afloat. She thought of Conrad and Mrs Wright and she wondered if she might have handled things better the day before. A frown puckered the smooth line of her brow. Only a spineless creature wouldn't have done what she had. There was no way in the world she would have allowed Mrs Wright to sit in that dusty bedroom one second longer than she already had. And Mrs Wright's bathroom had needed a good cleaning. Flora had said she was too busy so Marnie had offered to clean the bedroom and the bathroom, considering it all part of her job. And that meal! Marnie's stomach twisted at the memory. That chicken was definitely off!

Poor Mrs Wright! The dear old lady had actually enjoyed helping Marnie with the cleaning and while they had worked Mrs Wright spoke to her of the early days when she had been in full command of the house.

'Of course servants in those days took pride in their work,' she had told Marnie. 'And they came to you properly trained.'

'Whatever happened to them?' Marnie had asked.

'Oh, they've all passed on or they've retired. How I miss them,' she had sighed. 'Flora and Annie have been with us for just six months and I haven't had the strength to train them, so it's really not their fault that they are so poor at their jobs. Staff are so hard to find nowadays,' she had confided to Marnie, 'that once you get somebody you daren't lose them. It seems to me you cater more to them than they do to you. Not like the old days. Things were different back then.'

'But surely you don't need two full-time maids. Wouldn't a good housekeeper once or twice a week be better than those two?'

Old Mrs Wright shook her head. 'I have a bad heart and with Conrad away so often, he insists that I have someone around all the time. With two, one can have time off while the other stays and only one ever goes shopping at a time.'

'I wonder if my aunt would know of someone?' Marnie had mused aloud. 'She hears things in the shop. I'll speak to her about it.'

Mrs Wright had become agitated. 'Oh, no!' she had exclaimed. 'It was difficult enough finding Flora and Annie. If they think we're trying to replace them they might quit.'

So, Marnie had thought, it was a simple case of 'better the devil you know than the one you don't!' For Mrs Wright's peace of mind she had let the matter drop. At least while she was here she could take care of the old lady. When she had gone . . .? She tried not to think about it.

Marnie rolled on to her stomach and let the waves ride her ashore. She stretched out on her towel to let the sun dry her. Her thoughts wandered to Conrad. It was obvious he cared deeply for his grandmother, doing what he could to make her life easier. He honestly believed his grandmother was being well taken care of. Mrs Wright had been properly groomed when he had driven her into the city to do her Christmas shopping and Marnie knew enough now to know that Mrs Wright would never complain about Flora and Annie, mainly because she didn't want to put any more problems on an already overworked grandson, but also because she was afraid of being left alone.

Yesterday, when Mrs Wright was cleaning out her desk, she came across a book belonging to Conrad and which she had borrowed 'ages ago', she had said, and asked Marnie if she would return it to his room. When Marnie had gone into his bedroom to return the book she couldn't help but notice how immaculate Conrad's bedroom was in comparison to his grandmother's. Naturally he would have assumed Flora and Annie were looking after his grandmother's in the same manner. Oh, it was so easy to deceive, Marnie had thought ruefully.

A shadow crossed over her, blocking out the sun. Marnie's eyes flew open and she blinked up at Conrad standing over her. She quickly got up, bracing herself against any criticisms which might be forthcoming due to the fact she was sunning herself on the beach instead of being up at the house with his grandmother.

But instead of reproaching her, Conrad merely smiled down at her upturned face and Marnie felt the tension leaving her body.

'You're up and about early,' he drawled in a charmingly relaxed manner. 'It's not often anyone beats me to the beach.'

He was wearing red surfboard shorts and Marnie couldn't help noticing they were an identical red to her bikini. Beside him stood a long tapered surfboard, one hand supporting it. His sun-bronzed muscles rippled under the satin smoothness of his skin and silky black hairs formed a T across the broad expanse of his chest and down to the waistband of his board shorts. He was by far the most exciting male specimen she had ever seen, or was ever likely to see!

'Tomorrow I might not be up quite so early,' she said with a grin, her eyes leaving his to gaze at the surfboard.

'Would you like a go?' he asked, tilting the board towards her.

Marnie drew back, her grin widening, showing perfect white teeth. 'No, thank you! The last time I tried that I misjudged a wave and almost drowned beneath tons of swirling foam!'

His answering chuckle washed over her, making her feel warm and effervescent inside. 'The board's too large for you anyway,' he answered, his black eyes running appreciatively over her slender figure, perhaps resting a fraction too long on the soft curves of her breasts. But for some reason Marnie didn't find this offensive. She knew the difference between being leered at and being openly admired and Conrad was openly admiring her, making her feel glad and proud that she was a woman.

His gaze shifted to the rolling surf and Marnie's eyes followed his. Far from shore the great, monstrous waves reared up like towering walls, riding closer and closer to shore before crashing down and splintering into great howling booms like the sides of mountains suddenly exploding. Marnie shivered. The huge surf was caused by the King Tides which swept along Australia's eastern coastal beaches at Christmas and were sometimes called the Christmas tides. Only the bravest and most experienced board riders dared ride them.

'Do you think you should?' Marnie asked, an odd quake to her voice.

But he didn't hear her. He was listening to the sound of the waves and she saw by the set of his jaw and his rigid profile that the waves were beckoning to him and that he was determined to accept their challenge. He lifted his board and she watched him get it into the water, waiting for a wave to break before getting on to it so he could paddle out in relative safety. Marnie knew that if the board and its rider somehow managed to get under the mountain of water, the sheer weight of it would smother the rider before he had a chance to surface. Her heart caught in her throat as she watched him paddle into a wave as it rose like a giant slide, managing to keep ahead of it before it dissolved into foam.

He was out in the distance now and she saw him looking over his shoulder as a mountainous wave sped towards him. Let that one go! she silently prayed, as the terrifying wall of water loomed over him. He rose on his board and with the ease born of a natural athlete he rode the wave expertly, riding the crest, dipping and curving, his feet stepping across the waxed board as he steered it, taming the wild monster, beating it until it was nothing but a pool of foam gasping close to shore and then disappearing against the sand. Marnie watched him slide behind the comber and then ride to shore behind it in the relative calm of its passing. She had never seen such a beautiful piece of surfing so expertly executed, and her eyes were shining as she raced to the water's edge to greet him.

He dragged the board after him, keel up, and reached for the towel Marnie had brought him, smiling roguishly down at her as he wiped the salt water from his face and hair, dragging it across his chest before tossing it carelessly over one broad shoulder. There was a wild, triumphant gleam in his eyes and she knew it was because for a few precious moments man and sea had become as one and for a brief space in time he had been free of responsibilities and of commitments. He had been a wild thing.

They walked back to the house and he told her how he had taught himself to surf-ride just from watching the surfies when he had been a small boy.

'I bought my first board with pocket money I had saved up from doing chores,' he laughingly confided. 'I was all of seven and the board I bought was way too big for me but I still managed to learn on it despite the many bumps and bruises I received in the process.'

She loved listening to him, his voice deeply pleasant in his carefree mood, so different from the other times he had spoken to her, when his voice had been harsh and accusing. It was almost as if they were friends. Good friends! Marnie found herself telling him how she had bragged to a boyfriend when she was fourteen that she could ride the waves and how she had almost drowned trying to prove it.

'That was a long time ago and in calm waters. I've learned to ride fairly well since then but I would never attempt a surf like this!' She shuddered at the very thought.

'I suppose a girl like you would have plenty of boyfriends,' he said and Marnie looked up at him, wondering at the sudden change in his voice.

'What is that supposed to mean . . . a girl like me?'
And her own voice became guarded as she realised that
their carefree mood had gone and that they were both
on the defensive.

They were at the house now, standing on the
flagstone patio beside the french doors leading into the
sun room. He leaned the surfboard against the brick
wall and looked down at her. Her chin was raised in
defiance as she awaited his reply.

'Well, you're extremely outgoing for one thing,' he
drawled, his penetrating gaze leaving her face to sweep
down the length of her body. 'A beautiful face and a
figure to match.' He shrugged a dismissal. 'You must
have to beat the men off with sticks!'

Marnie's cheeks were scarlet. 'I've had my fair share
of boyfriends,' she admitted, truthfully enough, but
managing somehow to sound guilty about the fact. She
felt her composure slipping and she suddenly felt
extremely young and vulnerable and wished she had
remembered to bring her beachrobe with her so she
wouldn't have to stand in front of him dressed only in
her bikini.

His black gaze held her violet blue one and behind them
the grandfather clock ticked away in a corner of the sun
room, time marching on oblivious to Marnie's heart
which had seemed to stop beating in her chest as Conrad
held her in the magnetic hold of his powerful dark eyes.

Finally he drew himself up to his full towering height,
his breath escaping from tightly compressed lips and it
wasn't until Marnie released her own breath that she
realised she had been holding hers as well. Confusion
clouded her eyes and she bent her head, her teeth
clenching on her bottom lip.

'Shouldn't you be upstairs getting my grandmother
ready for breakfast?' he asked sharply, and Marnie's
head lifted and there was fresh defiance in her eyes.

'Yes, of course!' she answered stiffly, turning on her heel and marching through the french doors and across the sun room, feeling with every step she took that his eyes were boring a hole in her back.

Upstairs in her room she stared at herself in the mirror. She looked like a dishevelled child, her cheeks flushed and her hair mussed from the wind and the surf. Her eyes were burning as if from fever and she felt hot tears pricking behind her lids.

What had gone wrong? she thought dismally. One minute they were chatting and laughing and the next they were regarding each other like foes. Did he think that because she had had boyfriends that she wasn't a suitable companion for his grandmother, that she might use his home as a courting place for her beaus? The idea was preposterous and it would even be laughable if he hadn't looked at her in that coldly critical way which always managed to make her feel defensive and awkward.

Marnie took a quick shower and dressed in a pair of tight-fitting pink jeans which he would probably disapprove of and which she had deliberately chosen to wear knowing he would. She topped the jeans with a matching pink sleeveless top which showed off her golden tan and which also effectively outlined her curves. Brushing her hair into a smooth cap and applying a dab of pink lipstick, she was ready.

Her wrist watch was on her dresser and she slipped it on, noticing the time was seven. Still early, but late enough to waken Mrs Wright. Marnie took a few minutes to make up her bed and tidy her room before going into Mrs Wright's room. She would draw a bath and help get her dressed and then they would go downstairs for breakfast. No more of this eating by yourself in the bedroom. At least not while she was here!

But Mrs Wright wasn't in her room when Marnie opened the door. The bed had been made and there was the odour of lavender soap drifting from the opened bathroom door indicating Mrs Wright had already taken her bath. Annie came out of the bathroom carrying damp towels across her arm.

She stopped when she saw Marnie and she became flustered at Marnie's openly quizzical stare.

'Mrs Wright is downstairs having her breakfast,' Annie quickly stammered. 'She's had a bath and I helped her get dressed,' she added as though this was the usual practice and care the old woman received. 'Mr Wright stopped by just a few minutes ago and collected her. They've gone down for breakfast together.'

'Well!' Marnie exclaimed, her eyes rounded in surprise. 'Well, thank you, Annie,' she said, her eyes sweeping around the room, It had been thoroughly cleaned yesterday but there was a vacuum cleaner sitting in the middle of the floor and beside it was a trolley laden with cleansers and polishers. Annie dropped the bath towels into a laundry bag and Marnie could see that the sheets had also been changed, even though she and Mrs Wright had changed them yesterday and Marnie remembered how soiled they had been, evidence that clean ones hadn't been put on the old woman's bed for quite some time. Now here they were being changed twice in two days. It just didn't make sense. Or did it?

Marnie made her way slowly downstairs. Voices came from the sunny breakfast room just off the dining room and she met Flora carrying a tray in that direction and she fell into step behind her.

Mrs Wright was sitting at the table with Conrad at the head, looking relaxed and totally at ease, dressed casually in a pair of beige slacks and an open-necked shirt of the same colour. He was chuckling over something his grandmother had just said and Mrs Wright looked happy and pleased that she had managed to amuse her grandson.

They both looked up when Marnie appeared. Conrad's eyes swept over Marnie's outfit but he said nothing, rising to his feet and pulling out a chair for her to sit upon.

'Thanks,' Marnie murmured as she took the proffered chair. She smiled across at Mrs Wright and the old lady beamed back at her. She was obviously in her element, her snow white hair brushed neatly into a chignon and the powder blue dress she was wearing suiting her pale skin.

Flora put down the tray she had been carrying and removed the lid from a serving dish. Fried eggs, ham, bacon and potatoes were arranged neatly on the tray surrounded by freshly grilled tomato halves topped with a crispy cheese. Flora had certainly outdone herself Marnie thought, mentally comparing this meal with the burnt toast which had been Mrs Wright's breakfast the morning before.

'Why that looks lovely, Flora!' Mrs Wright smiled up at the housekeeper. 'I trust you kept out some for yours and Annie's breakfast?' she enquired in a kindly manner.

'Annie and I ate much earlier on, Mrs Wright,' Flora said as she collected the orange juice glasses, a smug look on her face as she watched Marnie drain the last of the freshly squeezed juice from her glass. Marnie handed the glass to her, her violet coloured eyes darkening at the sight of that look as Flora took her empty glass and then proceeded to leave the room.

The platter was handed round, each one serving themselves from the delicious assortment, but Marnie found she had little appetite. Conrad and his grandmother chatted through the meal and Marnie was aware of Conrad's eyes on her on several occasions. At last the meal was over and they settled back with steaming, fragrant cups of coffee, and Marnie waited for Conrad to begin the questioning he had promised concerning his grandmother's care at the hands of Flora and Annie.

He leaned back in his chair, coffee cup cradled in his large brown hands. 'Well, Grandmother,' he began, his voice gentle as he addressed the elderly woman. 'How have Flora and Annie been treating you?'

'Why, whatever do you mean, dear?' Mrs Wright asked, puzzled.

Conrad glanced across at Marnie. She met his gaze unflinchingly. He turned back to his grandmother.

'Marnie seems to think you've been neglected,' he continued in his kindly voice. 'If that's true then I want you to tell me.'

Mrs Wright turned to look at Marnie and Marnie saw the pleading look in her eyes. A look which begged Marnie not to cross her, not to say anything which would shatter the peace.

She turned back to her grandson. 'Marnie's such a kind and gentle girl,' she said. 'But I do believe she's a worrier ... like my sister Kate used to be,' she added seriously and Conrad nodded and smiled at his grandmother as they both remembered Kate.

'Are they keeping your bedroom clean?' he asked then.

'Why, of course. You saw Annie in there this morning vacuuming it out and dusting. Such a conscientious girl.'

'And your meals? Are they nutritious?'

'Very much so!' And Mrs Wright nodded her head emphatically.

'What did you have served to you last night?' he enquired casually, his eyes watching Marnie as she turned various shades of red.

His grandmother frowned, trying to remember. She brightened. 'We had an omelette. Yes, that's what it was, an omelette.'

'Marnie said chicken was served to you.'

'Oh! Yes, I guess it was chicken.' Again she frowned, turning to Marnie. 'But I seem to remember an omelette.'

Marnie opened her mouth to speak but Conrad held up a warning hand, effectively silencing her.

'You did have omelette,' he said gently, 'but that was after Marnie returned the chicken to the kitchen. The chicken was bad.'

An understanding light flashed briefly in his grandmother's eyes. Again pleading eyes were turned on Marnie and Marnie bowed her head, pity swelling her heart for this poor, frightened woman.

'Of course the chicken wasn't bad!' Mrs Wright scoffed at the suggestion. 'Flora would never give me something bad. Why just think of the breakfast we have just eaten. It was delicious!'

'Why didn't you eat the chicken then?' Conrad pressed on, his eyes watching his grandmother's face.

'The meal looked too heavy,' she replied, promptly. 'I preferred something light.'

'Like an omelette?' he quizzed.

'Yes,' she answered.

Marnie looked up at the silence which followed. Conrad and his grandmother looked pleased ... and relieved!

Flora came in to collect the coffee cups. There was a pleased expression on her face as well. Marnie wondered how much, if not all, of the conversation she had heard.

Marnie looked at the three of them. Only old Mrs Wright's eyes had kindness in them as they returned her gaze.

CHAPTER THREE

MARNIE and Mrs Wright wandered through the landscaped gardens after breakfast. Conrad had already departed for the day and Marnie suspected that even though it was barely eight o'clock this was a late start for him. He had kissed his grandmother goodbye and told her he wouldn't be home until late tomorrow evening, that he was having problems on one of his construction sites. He had nodded at Marnie and offered her a curt 'goodbye'. She had offered him the same, in the same manner.

Marnie and Mrs Wright headed towards a white painted cane bench in one corner of the garden, shaded by a clump of umbrella trees and surrounded by a bed of lovely red roses.

Mrs Wright leaned back against the bench, her eyes closed and a peaceful expression on her face. She was totally relaxed. Her eyes opened and she looked at Marnie sitting next to her and she reached across and patted Marnie's hand.

'Don't be cross with me, dear,' she said. 'I had to let Conrad think that everything is all right. When you get old you might understand how dreadful it is being a burden on someone.'

Marnie was turned towards her and she clasped the old lady's hands in her own. 'Dear Mrs Wright,' she spoke softly, 'Conrad doesn't think you are a burden. He's concerned about your welfare and wants you to be happy. It's not right to pretend that everything is fine when it's not. It's not fair to your grandson and it's certainly not fair to yourself.'

'But I have you now,' Mrs Wright said. 'So everything is going to be all right.' She smiled happily and again leaned back, closing her eyes. Marnie stared at her helplessly. Mrs Wright was pretending again. She was pretending Marnie would be here forever just like she had pretended Flora and Annie were being good to her.

Bees hummed in the quiet morning air, gathering pollen from the flower beds. Bush canaries flew above them and humming birds hovered over the flowering shrubs. Across the sweeping lawns the sound of the surf thumped a gentle beat against the sand, while seagulls swooped and dove into the sea.

Marnie leaned back against the bench and sighed. It was so beautiful here and she wondered what it would be like to stay here indefinitely. Her eyes flew open and she silently scolded herself. She was starting to pretend just like Mrs Wright!

While Mrs Wright was having an afternoon nap, Marnie rang her aunt, briefly describing the situation, explaining why she had decided to take on the job for the whole of the summer.

'I thought there was something terribly wrong there,' her aunt commented knowingly.

'Do you think you could keep your ears open at the shop, Auntie?' Marnie asked. 'You never know, you might hear of someone who's looking for a housekeeping job and who wouldn't mind looking after Mrs Wright.'

'What about that agency you went to?' her aunt asked. 'Wouldn't they have housekeepers listed in their books?'

'No, they're mostly a babysitting agency and companions for the elderly is just a small part of their business.'

'Well, if I hear of anyone I will certainly let you

know,' her aunt promised. 'Will you be able to make it for Christmas dinner? We eat at seven you know.'

Marnie hesitated. 'I don't know what the plans are for here,' she said, 'and Conrad is expecting a lot of guests.' But would his grandmother and herself be included for Christmas dinner she wondered. 'If I'm able to come would it be all right if I brought Mrs Wright with me?' Marnie asked.

'Yes, of course,' her aunt answered. 'It would be a pleasure.'

When Marnie hung up the telephone she went into Mrs Wright's room to find she had awakened from her nap. For the rest of the afternoon they wrapped the gifts Mrs Wright had purchased from Marnie's aunt's shop. Her aunt only stocked high quality merchandise and as Marnie had been the one helping Mrs Wright make her selections she already knew what the gifts were, but not who they were for.

Now she found that the wallet, the tie clip, the monogrammed handkerchiefs and a gold chain were for her grandson. The two leather handbags were for Flora and Annie but the gift which had caused the most trouble was a beautiful diamond pendant hanging on a gold chain. The pendant had cost a small fortune and Mrs Wright had looked at several before finally deciding on this one.

Mrs Wright held the jewellery box in her hands and Marnie could see she still wasn't sure if she had made the right selection. The pendant sparkled against the blue velvet lining and Mrs Wright touched it, shaking her head.

'I wish I could be certain Helena will like this,' she sighed, passing the box and its contents to Marnie. 'Would you like it if you received it as a gift?' she enquired anxiously.

'The pendant is beautiful,' Marnie assured her, 'and

it's one of a kind, designed by my uncle, and the craftsmanship is beyond reproach.' She handed the box back to Mrs Wright. 'Why are you so anxious about this particular gift? You have no reason to be, you know. Any woman would be thrilled to own it.'

'But you don't know Helena Wilcox,' Mrs Wright sighed, reaching finally for a piece of wrapping paper in which to wrap the gift.

Marnie met Helena the following evening when Conrad arrived home with her. She was tall, blonde and beautiful, and judging from the possessive way in which she held on to Conrad's arm she was also very much in love with the man.

Mrs Wright had retired early and Marnie had spent the evening in the sun room reading one of the books which lined the walls. The book had been exciting, an intriguing romance, and Marnie hadn't been aware of the time. It was only when she had heard footsteps and voices in the entry hall that she noticed by the grandfather clock that it was almost eleven o'clock.

Conrad and the blonde stood looking at her and Marnie stared back, startled by their sudden appearance, her mind still on the book.

'We saw a light on,' Conrad said, adding, 'It's late. Shouldn't you be in bed?'

Marnie was curled up like a kitten in a huge overstuffed armchair and now she uncurled her legs and got to her feet. She was dressed in a pair of white knickerbockers with a red and white striped T-shirt and she looked more like a teenager than the young woman of twenty-three that she was. She had kicked off her sandals and they were lying on the floor beside her chair. Marnie slipped her slender tanned feet into them and marked the page of the book she had in her hands. Her cheeks were a bright pink, caused more by the remark that Conrad had made about her being in bed than by the fact that the young woman was eyeing her with a great deal of curiosity. A curiosity which was far from friendly. There was a brittle hardness to the green eyes which focused themselves on Marnie and when Conrad introduced the two women, Marnie found she wasn't really surprised that this was Helena, and immediately thought of the diamond pendant which had caused Mrs Wright so much consternation.

'Helena will be here until after New Year,' Conrad was saying, his arm draped around Helena's shoulders, his smile lingering on her beautiful face. Helena smiled up at him, her heavily rouged lips inviting a kiss.

Marnie turned away as Conrad lowered his head and kissed Helena lightly on the mouth. Marnie's heart did a painful flip in her chest and she felt her stomach drop the way it did when she was in a lift. She walked over to the book shelf and put her book back, her fingers trembling as she slid the book into place. When she turned back Conrad was walking over to the liquor cabinet and Helena was draped into a chair, her knees crossed and the soft green chiffon dress she was wearing barely concealing her beautiful legs. She eyed Marnie with a slightly arched brow which Marnie knew was intended to make her feel somehow inferior.

'Conrad tells me you are a school teacher,' Helena drawled in a husky voice. 'School teacher turned nursing companion?'

So Conrad had discussed her with this woman, Marnie thought, not very happily. Did he feel he must explain her presence in his home in case Helena might object?

'No, I'm just here for the summer holidays,' Marnie answered as casually as her constricted throat would allow her.

Conrad turned from the liquor cabinet with two glasses of sherry. He walked over to Marnie and handed her one and she avoided his eyes as she took it, murmuring her thanks. He gave Helena the other and then returned to the cabinet where he picked up a glass of scotch. Sherry for the ladies, scotch for the men, Marnie thought, the little tune dancing around in her head making her feel dizzy. Or was it the sherry? She was amazed to see she had already drained her glass. Through the thick fringe of her lashes she saw Helena had barely touched hers.

Marnie walked over to the liquor cabinet and placed her glass down. Having finished her drink so quickly she felt she must justify her action. She swung back to Conrad who was watching her with curious amusement.

'Well, it's bed for me,' she said brightly, smiling at them both. 'I hope you enjoy your visit,' she said to Helena.

'I always do!' Helena assured her sweetly and Marnie's sensitive ears picked up a thread of warning which ravelled through the seemingly innocent words. Her smile faltered but she managed to hold on to it until she was safely out of the room.

Marnie saw light coming from under Mrs Wright's door when she got upstairs. Thinking something might be wrong, Marnie tapped lightly on the door. Mrs Wright's thin voice called out to come in and Marnie entered. Mrs Wright was standing in the middle of the room, her dressing gown on. She appeared agitated.

'Is something wrong?' Marnie asked, going immediately towards her. 'Why are you out of bed? Can't you sleep?'

'I thought I heard Conrad's car. Has he come home?'

'Yes, about twenty minutes ago. He's downstairs having a drink.' Marnie peered at her anxiously. 'Do you want to see him? I'll go and . . .'

'No, no, don't disturb him!' She looked up at Marnie, twisting her thin hands nervously. 'I . . . I suppose he's brought Helena with him?'

'Yes, she's downstairs with him now.'

Mrs Wright sighed. 'I knew she would be. He said he would be picking her up at the airport tonight.'

Marnie frowned. Was it possible that Mrs Wright was *afraid* of Helena? and then immediately dismissed the absurd thought from her mind. But as she remembered Helena's hard green eyes, an involuntary shiver raced up her spine. Was this the reason for Conrad saying his grandmother gets in the way when he had guests? Could it be that Mrs Wright and Helena clashed? Marnie decided she had better keep Mrs Wright out of Helena's way as much as possible during her visit. Marnie settled her into bed and stayed with her until she was asleep.

The next morning Marnie awoke early as was becoming her habit and was soon dressed in her bikini, a bright yellow one this time, and making her way down to the beach.

The water close to shore seemed much rougher today, chopping and churning, and Marnie could see the beach had been hollowed out and that it shelved steeply, the work of the King Tide. She decided not to enter the water here and turned to walk along the beach, hoping to come to a calmer patch. A soft breeze whipped up her short black hair, lightly tousling it. She broke into a little run, feeling light-hearted and free, loving the feel of the sand against her bare feet. The morning sun splashed against her cheeks and warmed her body.

About one hundred metres down the beach the water was much calmer and Marnie raced into it, diving through the waves like a slippery eel. She surfaced and pushed her hair back from her eyes, thoroughly enjoying herself, sensing that with Helena a guest in the house, her moments at the beach would probably be her only relaxed ones. Treading water, Marnie looked up the beach. She could make out the tall, muscular body belonging to Conrad as he stood on the dunes and looked down at the surf. He was like a bronzed statue, standing rigidly erect and Marnie felt her heartbeats quickening at the sight of him. He didn't have his surfboard with him. The waves were too choppy for board riding.

He turned his head and looked down the beach. Marnie stuck her arm out of the water to wave to him. She saw him shade his eyes with his hand and then his hands were cupping his mouth in the manner of someone shouting a message. Marnie smiled and waved her arm harder. He had seen her but why was he shouting? It was impossible to hear above the waves and from such a distance. Surely he would know that. She dropped her arm and started to swim back to shore. Perhaps Mrs Wright needed her, although Marnie felt certain she would still be sleeping.

Suddenly the water seemed to give way beneath her. Marnie stroked harder but the surf was pulling her away from the shore. She realised too late that she was caught in a strong rip and that a rip was capable of pulling her so far from the shore that it would be impossible to get back. Momentarily she panicked and swallowed water. Her head went under and when she surfaced she was choking and spluttering, which caused her to swallow more of the salt water. Frantically she tried to calm herself, to remember all the rules to follow if ever you were caught in a rip. She decided not to fight it but to allow herself to be dragged until the water released her. This way she would preserve her strength and hopefully ride a wave back to shore. But the undercurrent caused by the swell which had banked up and then flowed back to sea was much stronger than she had guessed. The rip pulled her with such force that she was dragged under. For the first time, as Marnie struggled to fight her way back to the surface, she faced the possibility that she might drown. Her lungs were bursting but the harder she tried to reach the top the deeper she seemed to descend. She had begun to lose consciousness when suddenly an arm appeared through the green swirling waters and she was propelled up to the surface. Gasping for air, her throat stinging along with her eyes and nose, she wasn't even aware that her head was out of the water, that she could breath. All she knew was that she *was* breathing and never had air seemed so precious, so grand, so miraculous!

Conrad held her in his arms until her choking had subsided, both his arms locked around her as he treaded water for them both. She felt the rapid beating of his heart and she felt wonderfully warm and *safe*! Never had she felt so safe, so warm. She rested her head against his shoulder and he allowed her to keep it there, one of his hands moving up to stroke her head. Marnie closed her eyes as he bent his head towards her, his lips a soft caress against her cheek. The warm protective feeling disappeared as another feeling moved in to take its place. She became aware of his body against hers, of a thrillingly exciting feeling sweeping through her, warming every nerve, igniting it into flame.

She stirred against him, lifting her head, her eyes questioning as she met his gaze. His eyes had never seemed so black, so fiercely potent. Her lips were parted and his mouth was almost touching them, a bee hovering over honey. His lips brushed hers as lightly as a feather but her world exploded into a trillion firecrackers all going off at once and each one a different, vibrantly beautiful colour.

Then he shifted her in his arms and before she realised what was happening she was on her back and he was swimming with her to shore as easily as if she were nothing but a rag doll.

He carried her from the surf and set her down on the

beach. Her legs felt wobbly beneath her and a strange silence settled around them, broken only by the lapping of the waves against the sand. She looked up at him uncertainly, conscious of his almost naked body so close to hers. His eyes were gleaming down at her and she was startled by the rage she saw in them.

'Can't you read?' He grabbed her arm and swung her around. In front of them was a huge sign. 'DANGEROUS RIP—SWIM AT OWN RISK'. Marnie stared at the sign. She had walked right past it without seeing it. 'I'm sorry,' she said, her voice husky sounding from her raw throat. She put a hand up to her neck. 'I just didn't see it.'

'Didn't see it!' he roared, his hands on his hips as he glared down at her, and she winced at the burning harshness which shone from his eyes. 'It's practically the size of a theatre screen! Are you blind?'

'Of course not!' she answered tightly, her throat becoming sorer by the minute. 'I wasn't looking for signs, I was looking at the water.'

His hands reached out unexpectedly and grabbed her shoulders shaking her. 'Do you realise how close you came to drowning?' he rasped angrily. 'If I hadn't spotted you when I did, you would be dead!'

Marnie shivered, remembering how it felt swirling helplessly in the rolling seas. Her eyes rounded with renewed fright. 'Yes, I know. Th-Thanks for saving me.' She whispered in a croaking voice.

'Thanks!? Is that all you can say . . . thanks?' He gave her another shake. 'I can't believe anybody, never mind a school teacher, could be so bloody careless. You almost drowned!' he repeated again with renewed rage.

Tears sprang into Marnie's eyes. 'I said I was sorry! What else do you expect me to say except . . . except sorry and thanks?' she was shivering with shock and reaction.

The anger seemed to leave him as suddenly as it came. He relaxed the cruel grip he had on her shoulders, his hands sweeping down her arms, to hold her hands. And then he cradled her in his arms, holding her gently, warming her, reassuring her, his hands softly stroking her, his fingers running through the dark, silky softness of her hair. She felt him trembling.

'Let's get you home,' he whispered against her ear. 'A hot bath and a rest is what you need right now.' With his arm tucked around her, he led her back up the beach, and she marvelled how nicely she seemed to fit under his arm as though he had been made just for her. Stop it! she scolded herself. You're pretending again. This man was made for Helena, not for you. The thought chilled her and she began shivering again. Conrad swooped her up in his arms and carried her the rest of the way to the house.

The household was quiet. Everyone was still in bed. Even so there was always the risk of someone getting up and if that someone happened to be Helena then Marnie figured she had better not be seen in Conrad's arms.

'Please, Conrad,' she murmured against him, her fingers lightly pressing against the silky black hairs which skirted across the broad muscular wall of his chest, 'You can put me down now. I can make it up to my room.'

He paid her no attention, his long legs moving swiftly across the sun room, down the long hall and up the stairs to her room. He bent down and turned the knob, pushing the door open with his foot and carrying her across to her bed. He laid her down and stood looking at her. Her chest was heaving as though she had run all the way from the beach instead of being carried. He smiled suddenly, his teeth gleaming white against the tanned smoothness of his skin. Marnie's heart somersaulted, and she licked her lips, which felt very dry. Every nerve in her body had been affected by that smile and she bowed her head in confusion wondering what on earth was happening to her.

'Stay put,' he drawled in an easy manner. 'I'll run your bath.' She watched him disappear into her bathroom and she lay without moving until he came back. The sound of running water filled the room and steam billowed out from the opened door. The sweet scent of hollyhocks drifted to her twitching nostrils and a smile curved her mouth because she knew he had added bubble bath to her water.

'Come on, mermaid,' he grinned, lifting her from the bed and carrying her into the bathroom. Her violet coloured eyes rested on the bottle of bubble bath. It was half gone!

'Good heavens!' she laughed, her eyes sweeping up to his face. 'You're only supposed to put a capful into the water, not practically the whole bottle!'

A devilish expression gleamed in his eyes. 'So, I got carried away.' His handsome mouth curved into a disarming smile as he bent his head and kissed the tip of her nose. Marnie's heart beat fast and hard and disappointment showed in her eyes because she had thought he would kiss her mouth, not her *nose*. Her lips had been parted in anticipation and now she closed them, wondering yet again at her strange behaviour. Maybe her brain had been starved of oxygen when she had almost drowned and this was why she was behaving so out of character. She had practically begged for his kiss and her cheeks turned scarlet when she saw the amusement light up his eyes. He *knew* she wanted him to kiss her! Embarrassment caused her to struggle in his arms and laughing softly he obliged by setting her down on the tiled floor. She turned her back to him and stared down at her bath water. The bubbles were piling higher and higher as the tub filled. He reached across her, bending down to turn off the taps. As he straightened, he scooped up a handful of the suds and plonked them on the top of her head. Marnie stared mutely up at him, but despite her resolve not to, she couldn't help but laugh. Her mouth dimpled at the corners and then she chuckled softly as the soft foam dropped on to her forehead and down the sides of her face. She bent quickly and scooped up a huge pile of the sparkling frothing bubbles and turned to throw them at him but he had anticipated her move and was already out of the door by the time she had turned.

'Coward!' she called after him.

'Have your bath,' he tossed over his shoulder before letting himself out of her bedroom.

Marnie blew the bubbles from her hands and watched as they flew about the bathroom, gradually dispersing into nothingness.

As she lay soaking in the warm water it felt as if Conrad was still with her. She could feel his presence in the room, could still hear the deep rumbles of his voice. Despite the sweet fragrance of the bath bubbles she was sure she could smell the heady male scent of him. She sighed and stirred restlessly in the water, remembering how it had felt when his arms were around her in the surf. His lips had barely touched hers but it had been enough to send her senses skyrocketing. Had he felt what she had? And then she laughed at herself, although no sound came from her lips. As if Conrad Wright would react like she had done over something as innocent and as brief as their kiss had been. You couldn't even really call it a kiss, Marnie reminded herself as she furiously scrubbed at her body as though trying to rid herself of the feel of his touch. He had said she looked like a student and here she was behaving exactly like a silly love-sick schoolgirl.

She stopped her scrubbing. Love-sick? Was it possible, she wondered? Was she in love with Conrad Wright? But no, of course not! How could she be? She barely knew him. She began scrubbing again, harder, faster, trying to rid herself of these ridiculously insane thoughts. It was probably a natural reaction because he had saved her life. It wasn't love she was feeling for him, it was gratitude! Yes, that's what it was. The thought made her feel better. It wouldn't do to be in love with a man she could never have, a man who had already been claimed by another woman. Helena's beautiful image sprang to her mind and immediately filled her with despair. She got out of the bath before she managed to scrub away her skin.

By the time Marnie had dried her hair and brushed it into its simple style, slipped into a soft pink sundress and matching pink sandals, it was time to awaken Mrs Wright. Conrad had suggested she have a rest but she knew she wouldn't be able to lie still for a minute. She had never felt more alive, or more restless.

Mrs Wright was awake when Marnie went into her bedroom, but she refused to get out of bed.

'Aren't you feeling well?' Marnie asked her anxiously.

'Just a bit down that's all,' Mrs Wright tried to explain and Marnie's straight brows knitted into a worried frown.

'You mean you're feeling depressed or ... or weak? Didn't you sleep well?'

'Not very well, I'm afraid. Just feeling a bit blue.'

Marnie sat on the edge of her bed and took one of the frail hands in her own. 'I know what it's like to feel like that,' she said softly, her blue eyes filled with sympathy and understanding. 'But after a bath you will be much better. I'll help you get dressed and then we can go downstairs for breakfast.'

'No!' Mrs Wright's eyes closed and Marnie felt sure

the old lady was trembling. Her eyes flew open and she looked anxiously up at Marnie. 'I don't want to have breakfast downstairs. I want to have breakfast up here . . . in my room.'

'But you know we took everything downstairs,' Marnie gently reminded her. 'We only have teabags up here. I don't even think there's milk.'

'A cup of tea will do me,' Mrs Wright declared, 'and I can drink it without milk.'

'Well, let's see how you are after you've had your bath and dressed. You'll probably feel like eating then, but if you don't I'll make us a drink and we can have it up here.'

It seemed to take forever before Mrs Wright was finally bathed and dressed and Marnie realised she was deliberately wasting time hoping, she suspected, that the breakfast being served downstairs would be well and truly over by the time she was ready.

'How do you feel now?' Marnie asked her when the last hair clip had been put into place. 'Hungry?' Her own stomach was howling for food.

'Not at all,' Mrs Wright answered stubbornly. 'A cup of tea will satisfy me.'

Marnie placed her hands on her hips. 'You're not going back to your old habits now that I'm here,' she told her firmly. 'If you don't want to dine downstairs then at least tell me why.'

'*She's* there!'

'Who?' And then understanding dawned. 'You mean Helena?'

Mrs Wright turned away without answering, her shoulders slumping. 'Yes,' she finally answered in a small voice.

Marnie frowned. 'But she's going to be here until after New Year! Surely you're not going to hide in your room until she leaves?'

Mrs Wright didn't answer. Marnie draped her arm around her thin shoulders. 'You've got me to lean on now,' she said softly. 'I'll be with you at the table.'

Mrs Wright leaned against her and then quickly moved away. 'I know what you're thinking. You think I'm a foolish old woman! You think I don't like Helena because she wants to marry my grandson. You think I'm deliberately trying to make a nuisance of myself so that Conrad will worry and fuss over me. You think I'm trying to put a rift between him and Helena so that they will never marry!'

Marnie stared at her speechless. She had never seen Mrs Wright so upset. Tears were streaming down her lined cheeks as she faced Marnie, a study in misery.

'I don't think any of those things,' Marnie told her gently. 'And I'm sure Conrad and Helena don't think them either.'

Mrs Wright looked at her helplessly, her eyes pleading with Marnie to understand, to believe her. Marnie chewed on her bottom lip wondering what she should do. She finally decided Mrs Wright was too upset to face eating in the dining room.

'Sit down and rest,' she said gently. 'I'll prepare us some breakfast and we'll eat it up here. Afterwards, we'll go for a drive. We can go to Manly and look at the shops.'

Mrs Wright sighed happily. 'That would be nice,' she said gratefully, drying her eyes on her hanky. 'We can have lunch there. We won't have to eat here!'

Marnie checked the smile which had started to form on her lips. 'Just today. Tomorrow we eat with the others in the dining room. I won't have you turning us both into recluses!'

When Marnie passed Conrad's study in the downstairs passage she could hear him barking orders into the telephone. As she passed the dining room she could see the table was set ready for breakfast. Approaching the kitchen she could hear laughter and then Helena's voice.

'Oh, you are a dear, Flora darling. How Mummy misses you, but just remember, it's all for a good cause! Too bad about that girl though. Couldn't you have stopped Conrad from hiring her?'

'Sorry, love. He announced it on us so sudden like. I told him there was no need but you know what he's like. Stubborn as a mule.'

'Well, she won't be here for long. She's . . .'

Marnie backed down the hall when she heard Conrad open his study door then, coughing lightly, she retraced her steps and entered the kitchen. Flora and Helena looked up at her in surprise. Helena's cold green eyes narrowed suspiciously on Marnie's face but her expression cleared when Marnie merely smiled at them both.

'Good morning,' she said brightly. 'Mrs Wright and I are going shopping so we won't be having breakfast here.' She walked over to the refrigerator and opened it. 'I'll just get us some juice and perhaps some of that bacon,' she said, closing the fridge door and carrying the juice over to a pan of bacon sizzling on the stove.

Flora and Helena remained silent as Marnie poured two glasses of juice and placed several strands of bacon on to a plate. Once more she smiled at them as she passed them on her way out of the kitchen. She met Conrad on his way to the dining room. He was freshly showered and shaved and looked cool and handsome in a pair of lightweight slacks and an open-necked white shirt. He frowned at the small tray she was carrying with their breakfast.

'What's this?' he asked. 'Why aren't you and Grandmother eating with us?' Was it her imagination or did he seem disappointed that he would be without their company?

'We're going shopping,' she explained a trifle nervously, still reacting from the conversation she had overheard. 'We'll get away faster if we just have something light upstairs.'

His eyes swept over her face. 'Do you think you should be shopping after your ordeal this morning? You don't look very well to me.'

'I'm fine,' she assured him, forcing a bright smile on her face. 'Just can't wait to go, that's all.'

'All right, then,' he said, reluctantly stepping aside so she could pass. 'But don't overdo it.'

'I won't,' she said and then asked, as if the thought had occurred to her. 'Who hired Flora and Annie?'

His black brows arched in surprise. 'I did of course.'

'But how did you find them?' she asked innocently. 'Help is so hard to come by nowadays.'

He flashed her a grin. 'Not when you have an expert looking for you.'

'An expert? Oh, you mean an agency.'

'Nope, I mean Helena. She found them for me!'

'Really?' Marnie pretended surprise. 'I wonder where she found them?'

Conrad shrugged his broad shoulders. 'How should I know? She found them and recommended them and that was good enough for me!'

But not good for your grandmother! Marnie thought as she made her way up to Mrs Wright's room. The hornet's nest was getting bigger and nastier by the minute.

CHAPTER FOUR

'IF you wait ten minutes I can drive you into town,' Conrad said as Marnie and his grandmother came down the stairs. Helena was standing beside him and she looked surprised and then annoyed at his offer.

'I didn't know you had planned to go into town,' Helena said looking up at him, and Marnie could see the angry glint in her eyes as she spoke.

'Something came up at the office,' he explained, not looking at her, but sifting through the pile of mail he held in his hands. He flashed Marnie a sideways glance. 'Will that suit you?' he asked.

'Well actually we hadn't planned to do our shopping in Sydney. We thought we would go to Manly.'

'I'll drop you off.'

'But how will we get back?'

'I'll pick you up.'

'But we don't know how long we'll be,' Marnie said, becoming exasperated.

He looked up from his mail. 'My business won't take long in Sydney. If you've not finished your shopping by the time I get to Manly I'll sit in the car and wait for you.' He looked at his grandmother. 'I'll park behind the post office. You can show Marnie where it is.'

His grandmother looked at Marnie. 'Let's go to Sydney, too,' she suggested brightly. 'We can stop in and see your aunt.'

Marnie hesitated. 'All right,' she agreed, aware of the murderous glance she received from Helena.

'That settles it then,' Conrad remarked as he started

towards his study with his pile of mail. 'Wait in the car, I won't be long.'

'I might as well come too,' Helena said and she rushed off to get herself ready.

Marnie and Mrs Wright were already settled in the back seat of Conrad's roomy Mercedes when he and Helena entered the garage. Conrad opened the door for Helena to get in and then he walked around to the driver's side, slipping in behind the wheel. No one spoke until they were on the open coastal road leading into Sydney. Helena broke the silence finally and continued to keep up a running dialogue until they reached Sydney. Marnie marvelled that Conrad had been able to concentrate on his driving through the busy traffic with Helena's constant prattle.

While they drove Marnie watched Helena, thinking of the conversation she had overheard between Helena and Flora. What had Helena meant when she said 'it was for a good cause' and what was Flora's connection with Helena? *Mummy misses you dreadfully.* What did that mean? Was Flora a relative? Or was she employed by Helena's mother and *lent* to Conrad? Conrad said Helena had found Flora and Annie but he didn't know *where* she had found them or *why*.

And what had Helena meant when she said 'too bad about the girl though'? There was no doubt that they meant her and it sounded as though they considered her to be in the way. In the way of what? Surely Helena and Flora didn't consider her a threat to Helena's and Conrad's relationship? What then? Were they planning something sinister? And did their plans have anything to do with Mrs Wright? Were they trying to wear her down by neglecting her and preventing her from eating properly? Were they trying to get rid of her by seeing that the poor soul was finally committed to an old people's home? Marnie shivered and stirred in her seat, trying to fight back her over-active imagination. She decided there was no sense in going to Conrad with her theories. He hadn't believed her last time and he would think her mad if she told him about her suspicions based on a snatch of conversation she had overheard. Better to wait and see what happened next. She would keep her eyes and ears open and watch Helena whenever Flora or Annie were around her. Helena had been on intimate terms with Flora in the kitchen. Marnie would see how she acted with Flora when Conrad was around.

Marnie's eyes wandered to the rear view mirror. She flushed when she saw Conrad's dark eyes watching her. His black brows were arched in a questioning manner and Marnie realised she had been frowning. She looked quickly away, sitting for the remainder of the journey with her face glued to the window and her thoughts whirling crazily around in her head.

Conrad parked the Mercedes in the parking lot behind his office building. Marnie wondered what Helena was going to do while he worked in his office. Or would she go up too and sit reading a magazine while he tended to his business?

The three women stood by watching while Conrad locked up the car. When he had finished he turned and smiled at them.

'It's not often a man has three beautiful ladies waiting for him,' he drawled, and all three women smiled dutifully.

'When should we meet you back here?' Marnie asked politely.

He glanced at his watch. 'One o'clock. That gives you three hours. Will that be long enough?'

'Yes, that will be fine,' Marnie answered, conscious of the glare Helena was favouring her with. Marnie took Mrs Wright's arm and they started to walk away.

'Marnie!' Conrad's voice.

Marnie turned around. 'Yes?'

'Don't you think you should invite Helena to go shopping with you? After all, she doesn't live in Sydney and doesn't know her way around.' There was no mistaking the reproachfulness in his voice. It was obvious he thought Marnie was deliberately snubbing Helena.

'It's all right, darling,' Helena smiled up at him, managing to sound pathetically brave about the whole thing. 'If Marnie *and* your grandmother don't want me tagging along then I'll just find something else to amuse myself.' She sighed and shrugged her shoulders, a picture of despair. 'I'll find a park bench to sit on or maybe I should just stay here and sit in the car.'

'Nonsense!' Conrad's black eyes flicked angrily over at Marnie and she could see the disgust in them that she could be so rude, so mean, as not to include Helena in their shopping expedition. She knew he expected her to invite her now.

'Please come with us,' Marnie spoke softly. 'It would give us an opportunity to get to know one another better!'

Helena looked sharply at Marnie, her green eyes narrowed in suspicion, but there was nothing in Marnie's face to suggest that she was being anything other than kind. Marnie's lips curved into a smile as she watched Helena, knowing what was going on in the other woman's mind. Yes, she felt like saying, I *did* hear you and Flora talking in the kitchen and I *do* want to know you and what you're up to. But of course she couldn't say this. It would have to be enough for Helena to think that whatever her little game was, it might no longer be quite so one-sided!

'There now,' Conrad spoke with relief, his dark head inclined towards Helena. 'You go along with Marnie and Grandmother and have a good time.' He put a large hand on Helena's shoulder and smiled down at her. A red hot spear of jealousy tore through Marnie's heart as she watched him with Helena and she felt physically sick in her stomach at the way in which Helena was simpering up at him.

'But mind you don't spend too much money,' he reminded Helena with a conspiratorial grin. 'Remember what you told me last night about your being on an economy drive.'

'I'll remember,' Helena promised dutifully, her bottom lip thrusted into a pout. 'But it's so terribly hard having to watch *every* penny, especially,' and here Helena looked meaningfully at his grandmother and Marnie, 'when *others* have so much to spend.'

Conrad chuckled and took his wallet from his hip pocket. Opening it he counted out several bills and handed them to Helena.

'Oh, Conrad!' she squealed delightedly, 'I didn't mean for you to give me money. I have ten dollars and . . .'

'Never mind,' he broke in, wrapping her fingers around the bills. 'Consider it a Christmas present in advance and enjoy yourself.'

Mrs Wright's face was showing open disapproval and her lips were pressed into a tight line, causing Marnie to wonder if this wasn't the first time Conrad had given Helena large sums of money. Marnie watched as Helena looked at the money greedily and then opened her handbag to stuff it inside. She wondered how any woman could be so lacking in pride as to practically beg money from a man in such a manner. And it wasn't as if Helena was poor. From her experience in her aunt's shop, Marnie recognised quality when she saw it. Helena's matching handbag and shoes must have cost a fortune, not to mention what the smart beige linen trousersuit she was wearing would have cost. She wondered how Conrad could be so gullible as to fall for her conniving ways.

Not that she cared, Marnie thought huffily. If Conrad wanted to play the fool then let him. It had nothing to do with her. Let him throw his money around if it pleased him. She couldn't care less!

Conrad looked across at his grandmother, his wallet still in his hands, and still opened. 'What about you, Grandmother?' he asked calmly. 'How are you fixed for money?'

'I have enough thank you, dear.'

He turned to Marnie and Marnie's chin jutted out defiantly as she looked scornfully down at his opened wallet, thinking he was about to ask her the same question. She would rather beg in the streets than accept money from a man who obviously enjoyed his role as 'sugar daddy'!

Conrad eyed her curiously and then guessing at what she was thinking, softly chuckled. He closed his wallet and tucked it back into his pocket. 'Make certain Grandmother pays for everything this time!' he said quietly, so that only she could hear. Marnie's face flushed a deep pink. He hadn't been about to offer her money at all. He had only turned to her to issue a warning.

'Of course,' she answered stiffly, the defiance still in her eyes as she glared up at him. She longed to wipe the smug look from his face. A look which told her quite clearly that not only had he read her thoughts but that he found it rather amusing that she should concern herself about his relationship with Helena.

The defiance left her eyes as she continued to stare up at him. She was aware of her heart thumping crazily as he held her gaze, and she forgot that they were standing in a parking lot and that his grandmother and Helena were with them. She forgot that only seconds before she had been quite angry with him. Confusion crept into the clear violet of her eyes, clouding them, as she teetered dangerously on the brink of drowning in the fathomless black pools of his eyes.

'Well?' Helena's voice separated them as effectively as if she had thrown a bucket of cold water over the two. Marnie shivered as she managed to drag her eyes from his, blinking across at Helena, almost without recognition. Helena's green eyes were focused on her, brittle with contempt.

'Conrad has work to do and I thought you wanted to go shopping,' Helena spat out crossly, as she went over to stand beside Conrad, separating him from Marnie.

Conrad had placed his briefcase on the bonnet of the car and now he turned to retrieve it, tucking it under his arm. Marnie could see he was already concentrating on the business which had brought him into town, the three women apparently forgotten as he quickly glanced at his wristwatch.

'Yes, I've got to be off,' he said, giving them a sweeping glance. His eyes rested for a fraction longer on his grandmother. 'Don't over-do things,' he warned her. And then he was off, leaving a trail of destruction in his wake.

Helena turned on Marnie immediately he was out of ear-shot. 'How dare you flirt with him?' she spat the words, eyes narrowed into evil slits. 'I saw the way you were looking at him with those big cow eyes of yours.'

'I'm surprised you can see anything at all,' Marnie returned sweetly. 'It must be hard looking through those dollar signs which are covering yours!'

'And what is *that* supposed to mean?' Helena enquired suspiciously.

'Nothing at all. Just a bit of tit for tat!'

Beside her, Mrs Wright shifted nervously and

immediately Marnie felt ashamed of herself. She was allowing Helena to drag her down to that girl's level. And there was nothing to be gained from it except upsetting Mrs Wright. Marnie straightened the shoulder strap of her bag and ignoring Helena, turned to Mrs Wright.

'Shall we go?' she asked, her smile assuring the old lady that everything was quite all right. Marnie tucked her arm into Mrs Wright's and, although it was a very hard thing to do, she turned back to Helena and said: 'What kind of shopping did you want to do?' she enquired politely. 'I can show you the best shops and . . .'

'You don't think for one minute that *I* would shop with *you*?' Helena interrupted Marnie. 'I'm quite capable of finding my own way around town without having to wait for you and *her*!' Helena's eyes swept over Mrs Wright in a manner which filled Marnie with a cold rage. Thankfully, Mrs Wright's attention had been diverted momentarily by a hair clip which had tumbled from the snow-white mound on to her collar, mercifully sparing her from Helena's cruel look.

'Why did you let on to Conrad that you wanted to come with us then?' Marnie couldn't resist asking. As if she didn't know, she silently answered herself. It was to put Marnie in a bad light in Conrad's eyes. Making it look just as Marnie had suspected, that poor Helena was being left in the cold when all she really wanted was to be dragged into the warmth.

Helena started to walk away. 'Figure it out for yourself!' she tossed over her shoulder, laughing sarcastically.

'Come on,' Marnie said, again taking hold of Mrs Wright's arm. 'If Helena gets lost, Conrad will blame me.'

But short of running after her there really wasn't

much Marnie could do. Mrs Wright was too old to run and Marnie didn't even dare make her walk quickly. Helena's long legs had already carried her out of the car park on to busy Castlereagh Street where the Christmas shoppers were out in throngs. Finding Helena would be like looking for a needle in a haystack. She could only pray that Helena wouldn't get lost and that she would remember to be back by one o'clock.

Mrs Wright's kindly face smiled up at Marnie. 'Don't worry about her,' she said. 'Helena is used to big cities. After all she does come from Melbourne.'

Looking down into Mrs Wright's face, Marnie remembered why they had come shopping in the first place. It had been to get Mrs Wright out of the house and away from Helena. Mrs Wright was her responsibility, not Helena. Surely Conrad didn't expect her to neglect his grandmother while she raced all over town trying to keep track of his girlfriend?

The three hours sped by quickly, most of it being taken up in the hairdressers after Mrs Wright had told Marnie she couldn't remember the last time she had visited a beauty salon.

'I used to go on a weekly basis,' she had confided while they had paused outside one of the busy salons. 'But now that I'm no longer able to drive I hardly ever go. Conrad would take me of course, but I don't like to ask him when he's so busy.' She sighed and looked wistfully in at the salon. 'I had planned to have my hair trimmed for Christmas but those days I came into town to shop, well, the time just seemed to slip by and besides,' she added mournfully, 'I kept forgetting to make an appointment.'

'Let's see if they can fit you in now,' Marnie suggested, and taking Mrs Wright's arm led her into the beauty salon. The salon was crowded but as luck would have it there had just been a cancellation and providing

Mrs Wright didn't mind having her hair done immediately, then the cancelled appointment could be hers. Mrs Wright was delighted and while she was being attended to, Marnie read magazines. When Mrs Wright was finally finished the wait had been well worth it. Mrs Wright looked stunning! Her hair had been cut into a fashionable style and waved softly around her cheeks. Marnie stood up when she saw her, a delighted smile on her face.

'Mrs Wright!' she exclaimed. 'You look absolutely beautiful!'

The old lady beamed with pleasure. 'Thank you,' she said, 'and you can stop calling me Mrs Wright. It makes me feel old! You must call me Eva.'

Marnie couldn't help noticing as they made their way to her aunt's shop, that Eva was constantly putting her hand up to feel her hair. as though reassuring herself that it had really been done.

'I think we should make certain you have your hair done once a week, again,' Marnie told her as they walked along. 'Is there a beauty salon in Palm Beach?'

'Why, yes there is and you have a car! Oh, it would be wonderful to go back to having my hair done professionally again.'

'Well, while I'm here, Eva,' and Marnie smiled when she said the name for she knew how Mrs Wright loved hearing her say it, 'I will make certain you get your hair done.'

When she and Eva stepped into her aunt's shop, her aunt stared at Eva in open-mouthed pleasure. 'Why Mrs Wright!' she greeted her happily, rushing over to clasp her hands. 'You look marvellous, such a change from the last time you were here!' Her aunt looked at Marnie and she smiled. warmly at her niece. 'You always were one to bring out the best in people.' Her aunt turned again to Eva. 'I do believe you've put on a little weight. And your hair! It's so becoming in that style.'

Eva stood and allowed herself to be admired, her pale cheeks colouring with pride and embarrassment, for it had been such a long time since anyone had openly complimented her. Her tired eyes sparkled with a new light and Marnie impulsively bent her head and kissed the lined cheek. Tears sprang to Eva's eyes, but she managed to smile through them, for they were really happy tears.

'I've just put the kettle on,' Marnie's aunt said. 'The girls are in the back making up some sandwiches and I think we have some cakes. Please stay.'

They had tea and cakes and afterwards when Marnie was helping her aunt carry away the cups, her aunt whispered: 'How are things *really* going?'

Marnie frowned as she remembered the conversation she had overheard that morning but she decided not to mention it to her aunt until she had found out more. Her aunt would only start worrying about her and if her aunt told her uncle then he might decide Marnie was in some sort of danger and demand that she leave. For Eva's sake, she realised her timing would have to be right, for if she let the cat out of the bag too soon then all chances of helping her would be lost.

'They're improving,' Marnie finally answered. 'Mrs Wright has the company she craved and she's been eating three good meals a day. And I get her out. She loves walking in the garden and she unburdens her heart to me. Conrad's father was her only child. He turned to drink and gambling after his young wife died giving birth to Conrad. The business suffered terribly and Eva thinks that's why Conrad drives himself so hard. To make up for what his father lost. The business ... and his wife.'

'Marnie?' Eva called out to her. 'We'd better be leaving. It's almost one o'clock.'

'Will you be able to come for Christmas dinner?' her aunt asked, including Eva in the invitation.

Marnie saw Eva's eyes widen in delight and she understood why. A new hairdo, a tea party and now an invitation for dinner! Eva looked expectantly up at Marnie. 'Let's!' she suggested hopefully and then turned to Marnie's aunt. 'But surely it would be too much trouble? You have your husband and your daughters to cook for. With two extra ...' Her voice trailed off waiting for Marnie's aunt to reassure her that it wouldn't be too much trouble at all.

Marnie spoke up before her aunt had a chance to answer. 'I'll find out from Conrad what the arrangements are. And I'll ring you tonight,' she promised her.

'Yes, I guess that would be the best thing,' Eva replied, nodding her head in agreement. 'Although we don't usually cook a big dinner. At least not a proper Christmas dinner.'

While Eva chatted with her two cousins, Marnie bought the gifts she had planned on beforehand and while her aunt was wrapping them, asked: 'Have you heard anything about a housekeeper yet?'

'Sorry, dear,' her aunt shook her head. 'I've made some enquiries but so far nothing has come from them. But I'll keep trying, don't you worry.'

'I know you will and ... and thanks for inviting us for dinner. It made Eva so happy to be invited somewhere. I haven't had a chance to discuss Christmas with Conrad yet, that's why I never mentioned your invitation to Eva before.'

'Oh, dear. I haven't done the wrong thing, have I?'

'Not in the least,' Marnie smiled. 'It thrilled her to be asked and even if we can't make it she will know she was invited.'

They were back at the parking lot for one o'clock. Marnie had been afraid Helena wouldn't get back on time, that she would somehow manage to get herself lost so that Conrad would blame Marnie for allowing her to go shopping on her own.

But as it turned out her fears were groundless. Helena was already back when they arrived and she was standing beside Conrad next to his car. Except for row upon row of vehicles the parking lot was deserted. Conrad looked up when they approached and Marnie saw immediately that he was extremly angry. His handsome features were gathered into a ferocious scowl as he glared at Marnie. Beside her Eva stood patting her hair waiting for her grandson to notice her new 'do'.

But Conrad was obviously in no mood to notice anything other than Marnie's face. She met his gaze squarely and then her eyes flew to Helena as she heard her sniff. It was obvious by Helena's reddened eyes that she had been crying. A hanky was clenched in her hand and she avoided Marnie's eyes as she dabbed at her own. Marnie's heart sank as she turned helplessly back to Conrad, her eyes pleading with him to believe that whatever had caused Helena to cry, she wasn't to blame. His answering look told her in no uncertain terms that he knew she *was* to blame!

The long drive back was one Marnie felt certain she would never forget. Eva sat rigidly beside her in the back seat of the grey Mercedes, the pleasure of her day spoilt by her grandson's dark mood. No one spoke, the occasional sniffle from Helena as she sat close to Conrad, being the only sound.

And each time Helena sniffled Marnie could feel Conrad's black eyes watching her from his rear-view mirror. She could feel his contempt, sense his anger and she knew that whatever Helena had told him, it must have been a whopper!

'I want to see you in my study,' Conrad rasped, as soon as they had arrived back and everyone was out of the car. Helena had run into the house still dabbing her eyes with the hanky and Eva was hurrying after her as if she too wanted to be well away from Conrad's wrath.

Marnie looked up at him and sighed. 'Yes, I thought you might.' She started towards the house. 'I'll be there in half an hour.'

He grabbed her wrist. 'NOW!'

His fingers were like bands of steel digging into the fragile bones of her wrist but not for the life of her would she give him the satisfaction of letting him know he was hurting her. Her voice was as quiet as his had been loud when calmly she said: 'A half hour!'

His black eyes widened in surprise that she would dare have the audacity to argue with him. The pressure on her wrist increased but still she held firm, her chin held high as she met the ferocity of his gaze. It was only when he released her that she said; 'Your grandmother is tired. I'll settle her down for a nap and *then* I'll come to your study.'

He jammed his hands into his slacks' pockets, his shoulders hunched forward as he peered at her beneath thick black brows. His lips were compressed into a thin white line as he fought to control his anger. Marnie felt a thrill of fear race down her spine and she was grateful his hands were safely tucked away in his pockets!

But as much as she wanted to turn and flee into the house she found she couldn't move. It was as if she was rooted to the spot she was standing on. Her blue eyes were locked once more to his in that strange magnetic hold that she seemed incapable of defending herself against. Currents of electricity sparked between them, fusing them into a common bondage which neither seemed capable of freeing themselves from. She heard a sharp hissing sound as Conrad released his breath. His mouth relaxed but didn't soften. Neither did the hard, angry look in his eyes lessen.

But the sound had been enough. It had broken the spell. Marnie was already turning to go into the house when he spoke.

'A half hour,' he warned. 'Not one second longer!'

Eva was already lying on her bed when Marnie got upstairs. As she slipped a blanket over her she smiled down at her.

'You must be tired,' she said gently. 'Have a nice nap.'

Eva closed her eyes and gave a contented sigh. She made no mention of Conrad or Helena and Marnie realised Eva had managed to erase the whole unpleasant episode from her mind.

In her own room Marnie had a quick shower, feeling hot and sticky from her trip into Sydney and changed into a cool candy-striped halter dress. She gave a silent prayer of thanks to her mother, from whom she had inherited her clear complexion which made it unnecessary for her to wear make-up. After brushing her damp hair quickly into place she was ready with minutes to spare.

She forced herself to walk calmly to his study, taking deep even breaths as she made her way down to whatever was awaiting her. I have done nothing wrong, she kept telling herself, so I have nothing to fear! Then why am I shaking like a leaf? she wondered dismally.

'Come in,' he growled when she knocked on the door of his study.

Her hand was trembling as she twisted the knob and stepped in. He was standing with his back towards her, staring out of the windows. The short-sleeved white shirt he was wearing stretched dangerously across the broad width of his back, emphasising powerful shoulders and equally powerful arms. A thin brown leather belt encircled his trim waist and narrow hips gave way to the strong columns of his legs held stiffly apart.

Marnie hesitated on the threshold and when he didn't turn she skitted across to the nearest chair sinking gratefully into it.

He turned slowly and she saw immediately that his anger had passed. Her relief was so great that she relaxed into the chair and a smile tugged at the corners of her mouth, unfortunately giving him the impression of a 'couldn't care less' attitude.

Fresh anger blazed in his eyes and Marnie immediately stiffened, her heart beating frantically as she watched the change in his face. He held a slide rule in his hands and she heard it snap as he broke it in two. Unconsciously, her hand slipped up to her throat and she held it there, her eyes glued to the broken fragments in his hands.

A sardonic smile twisted his lips as he watched her, and then he carelessly tossed the severed pieces into his wastepaper basket, one at a time. He walked over to his desk and leaned against it, long legs stretched out in front of him, ankles crossed, his feet almost touching hers as she sat in front of him.

'You just couldn't be nice to her could you?' he began in an ominously low voice. 'As soon as my back was turned you made a dig at Helena for accepting that money I gave her.'

Marnie had forced herself to look up at him but now she lowered her eyes, realising as she did so that he would take it as an admission of guilt. And if that didn't do it then the warmth flooding her cheeks certainly would. She stirred uncomfortably in her chair and studied her fingernails.

She heard his sharp intake of breath and then he let it out again in a long rasping sound. 'Nothing to say in your own defence, Marnie?' he asked cuttingly. 'Aren't you even going to deny saying to Helena that she had dollar signs for eyes?'

Oh, why had she allowed Helena to bait her, Marnie thought ruefully, wishing she had suffered the pain of biting her tongue rather than being forced to suffer through the humiliation of having Conrad throw her words back at her. She squared her shoulders and looked up at him.

'I did say something like that,' she admitted truthfully, knowing she had no one other than herself to blame for her present situation. 'But if you expect me to elaborate on the subject then you're wrong because I have no intention of doing so.'

She didn't see him move. There was more of an impression of something blurring in front of her before she was lifted from her chair. 'I'm sick of your "holier-than-thou" attitude!' he snarled, his fingers digging into the soft, bare flesh of her arms. 'You are under my employ and I trusted you to look after Helena who is my guest. Instead you insult her, making damned sure she wouldn't go shopping with you and Grandmother. And worse than that,' he continued, his head bent over her, giving her the full benefit of blazing black eyes, 'Helena tells me you are deliberately creating a rift between her and Grandmother!'

Marnie felt his grip in her arms lessen and she took advantage of this by quickly wrenching herself free, whirling the swivel chair around so that it stood between them. 'I refuse to be blamed for more than I've done,' she flared, her face pale except for two burning red flags high on her cheekbones. 'If there's a rift between your grandmother and Helena then it was there long before I arrived here. Furthermore,' she continued, her voice quivering, 'I don't believe Helena had the faintest intention of going shopping with us despite what she may have said to you.'

Marnie's hands were gripping the top of the leather chair, her knuckles white. The telephone on his desk jarred the silence as they stood glaring angrily at each other. He allowed it to ring several times before he reluctantly turned to answer it, his voice gruff as he spoke into the mouthpiece. By his words Marnie guessed it was a business call and by his tones realised there was a problem at one of his construction sites. She saw him run a hand through his hair, a weary expression on his face. Quickly he reached for a pen and as he began to jot some numbers on to a pad Marnie started to walk towards the door, but stopped and retreated to the back of her chair when he motioned for her to stay.

On his desk were several cylinders. He supported the mouthpiece of the telephone on his shoulder holding it in place with his chin while he used his hands to grab one of the cylinders, still speaking rapidly into the telephone. Without wondering whether her help would be appreciated, Marnie stepped forward and removed the blueprint from the cylinder which he had been struggling with and rolled it out on to his desk, holding it in place while he scribbled measurements on to it. He gave her a curt nod which she knew was his way of thanking her and an unexpected surge of pleasure soared through her being, making her feel she had done something monumental instead of just this one small deed.

For several minutes after he had replaced the receiver he stood leaning over his desk, his long fingers flying rapidly over a calculator as he worked out equations, setting the numbers of the formulas on the blueprint still rolled out in front of him.

Marnie watched him, fascinated by his power of concentration, and by the growing number of equations appearing on the blueprint. She knew he had quite forgotten that she was still in his office and when he looked up briefly to reach for another of his slide rules, he seemed almost startled by her presence.

Immediately he straightened, stretching and rubbing the cords at the back of his neck. She could see by the tense lines on his face that he was tired and she found herself hoping that he would manage to have some time off over Christmas.

'Sorry, Marnie,' he surprised her by saying. 'I wasn't being rude just now. Problems with a job,' he said, indicating the blueprint still sprawled across the shining surface of his desk. Even as he spoke Marnie realised his mind was still on his figuring, his earlier anger with herself forgotten or at least pushed to the back of his mind.

'Is there anything I can do to help?' she asked, wishing there was something she could do to relieve some of the pressures from his mind.

He removed his hand from the back of his neck and gave her a mocking glance. 'Just don't stir up any more trouble around here,' he said accusingly, 'and that will be help enough!'

Marnie stiffened but wisely held her tongue. She knew when he turned back to his desk that she had been dismissed, and she slowly crossed his study to stand watching him by the door.

'Your grandmother had her hair done at the beauty parlour this morning. She waited for you to notice it but you didn't and I think she was hurt. I think it would be nice if you complimented her tonight at dinner.'

He looked up impatiently, his black brows drawn together in a frown. 'What are you mumbling about?'

'Nothing,' she mumbled deliberately, hoping to annoy him.

But he had already picked up the telephone and was dialling a number, so he didn't hear Marnie's mumbled reply. She let herself out and softly closed the door, wondering as she heard the deep tones of his voice speaking into the 'phone why she had tried to annoy him when only minutes before she had wanted only to help him.

CHAPTER FIVE

When Marnie and Eva entered the dining room that evening for dinner, Helena and Conrad were already there standing by the elegantly carved buffet, a drink in their hands.

Conrad was dressed informally in a pair of maroon slacks topped with a black silk shirt. Marnie's breath caught in her throat at the sight of him. It seemed that each time she saw him he had somehow grown more handsome. His eyes met hers over the rim of his glass and a half smile formed on his lips as his gaze ran over her slender form dressed in a sleeveless jump suit of hunter green velvet.

He set his glass down and walked over to them, his eyes smiling down at his grandmother. Marnie saw him study Eva's new hair-do and she prayed that he would say something complimentary.

'You look different tonight, Grandmother,' he said in the gentle tones he used when addressing her. 'Your hair looks different,' he added teasingly.

Eva smiled and put both her hands on his arm. 'Do you like it?' she asked eagerly, only her eyes looking anxious as she waited for his reply.

He bent his head and kissed her cheek. 'Very much,' he assured her sincerely and Marnie smiled at them both as he covered his grandmother's hands with one of his own. Over the top of his grandmother's spanking new hair-do he caught Marnie's eyes and she saw that he was glad that she had told him about the 'do' even though she had thought he hadn't heard her.

With Eva's arm tucked in his he led her to the table

and sat her down on one of the high-backed chairs. Next he pulled out a chair for Marnie and then looked over to where Helena was still standing by the buffet. Helena was dressed in a shining gold off-the-shoulder dress, her long blonde hair flowing about her pale shoulders. As she walked towards Conrad's extended hand, the dress shimmered and swished as it was intended to do and Marnie had to admit, however reluctantly, that Helena looked a vision of loveliness. And she wasn't the only one to think so either, she saw with a sinking heart. Conrad's glittering black eyes spoke volumes as he took Helena's hand and guided her to her chair. Suddenly Marnie wished she hadn't worn her jump suit, that she had worn something a little more feminine. She thought longingly of the white chiffon dress hanging upstairs in her wardrobe and then immediately chided herself for her foolishness. Good heavens! she found herself thinking. Anyone would think I'm a contender in the race to win Conrad. Ridiculous! Absolutely ridiculous!

Eva picked up a small silver bell and gently shook it. A few minutes later Flora, followed by Annie, entered the dining room and set a tureen of soup on the sideboard. Annie ladled out the soup while Flora served it. Marnie watched discreetly while Flora served Helena, but there was absolutely no sign, not even the slightest gesture, that the two knew each other on intimate terms. Helena hardly spared Flora a glance as the soup was placed in front of her and even then the glance was impersonal. Flora might have been a waitress in a restaurant instead of the 'darling' she had been in the kitchen!

So intent was Marnie on her observations that she didn't notice Conrad watching her until his penetrating gaze got through to her. Her head turned as though drawn by a magnet, and she flushed at the look of devilish amusement which glowed from his eyes. His black brows were slightly arched in a half mocking manner and Marnie realised with a sudden horror that he thought she was watching Helena because she *envied* her!

Blushing furiously, Marnie dragged her eyes away and concentrated on her soup. Several minutes later she looked up to find she was the centre of attention and it was only then that she realised the chatter around the table had ceased.

'Yes? What is it?' she enquired generally, her eyes finally resting on Eva's kind face.

'I was just telling Conrad and Helena that you and I have been invited to your aunt's place for Christmas dinner,' Eva explained, her tired old voice quivering in anticipation.

Marnie smiled at her. At Eva's age not many of her colleagues were still around to issue invitations and Marnie guessed that it made Eva feel proud to be able to announce to Conrad and Helena that the 'old girl' was still in demand!

'Yes, that's right,' Marnie agreed, turning to Conrad. 'My aunt is planning on serving dinner at seven but I told her I would check with you first to see what the arrangements here would be.'

Conrad finished the last of his soup and pushed the bowl away before answering. 'Good thing you did,' he replied smoothly, but Marnie's sensitive ears picked up an underlying note of hardness, 'because the Wrights' always stay home for Christmas. It's part of our tradition.'

'But we haven't followed tradition for years, Conrad,' his grandmother smilingly reminded him, her tone indicating that she found it hard to believe that he could have forgotten this fact.

'Then it's about time we did!' His tone told them that

the subject was closed. Annie took away the soup bowls while Flora served baked fish and vegetables. The meal was delicious, but there was an uneasy current of tension which kept it from being enjoyable. It was almost as if Eva had announced she was leaving the country instead of just being away for a few hours enjoying a Christmas dinner. Even Helena, who had been chatting merrily was now noticeably subdued and because it had been Marnie's aunt who had issued the invitation, Marnie knew that in Conrad's eyes she was once again the culprit.

And incredibly she felt like a culprit! She was here to make things easier for Conrad and happier for his grandmother. Instead Eva was clearly unhappy about the invitation which had gone sour. Her head was bowed over her plate and she wasn't eating her food. Conrad was terribly annoyed, but at the same time Marnie saw concern in his eyes as he watched his grandmother.

Marnie looked down at her plate and was amazed to find it empty. Apart from the first bite she couldn't remember having eaten a thing. Like Conrad had done to his soup bowl, she pushed her plate away.

'Well,' she said brightly, hoping her cheerful smile looked better than it felt. Her face felt as though it had been turned to wood. 'What *are* the Wrights' traditions?' she folded her arms on the table and leaned forward, hoping her eagerness would be contagious.

It wasn't! They stared at her the way people do when they think someone is off their nut! Undaunted, Marnie continued, ignoring the faintly amused smile which appeared suddenly on Conrad's lips.

'What size tree do you usually get?' she asked, her lovely violet-blue eyes shining as she looked in turn at the three occupants sitting at the table. No one answered her. 'And the turkey! M-M-M-m-m-m! Don't you just love the fragrance of a big, juicy turkey baking for hours in the oven? That's what makes Christmas,' she declared with an emphatic shake to her head, 'a big tree with lots of decorations and a big turkey with all the trimmings.'

'Next you will be suggesting a sing-song around a pianola,' Helena remarked sarcastically. She turned to Conrad. 'Really, darling,' Helena gushed, 'wouldn't it be simpler to allow your grandmother and Marnie to go to Marnie's aunt's for Christmas dinner? After all, we have a lot of people arriving tomorrow and we certainly don't want to ignore our guests by chasing after Christmas trees and shopping for turkeys.'

'We haven't had a tree or a turkey in years,' Eva chimed in, sniffing into a lace handkerchief. 'Barbecues! That's all we ever have now,' she added in disgust.

Helena glared at her. 'A barbecue is far more sensible in this climate than roasting along with the turkey as it cooks!'

'Enough!' Conrad's voice seemed to boom around the table, even though he had spoken in a deathly quiet tone. He dragged one large hand wearily through his hair and it was clear to Marnie as she helplessly met his gaze that he held her responsible for the bedlam which had broken out.

Silence filled the room as no one dared speak. 'I . . . I'm sorry,' Marnie finally said, 'if I've . . . upset anyone.' She looked appealingly across at Conrad. 'I didn't mean to,' she added, hoping he believed her, but knowing he probably wouldn't.

Helena jumped up from her chair and raced around to Eva. Putting her arms around Eva's frail shoulders in a protective embrace, she looked across at Marnie with brittle green eyes.

'You've upset poor Mrs Wright,' she said accusingly. 'You've made her *cry*! How could you be so *cruel*?'

Helena didn't wait for an answer. The green eyes were turned on Conrad. 'Really, darling. This cannot be allowed to continue. First it was me this morning and now your grandmother! There's no end to the damage that girl causes.'

'So it would seem,' Conrad drawled, the handsome line of his mouth curving into a sardonic smile. There was an expectant silence in the room as they waited for Conrad to dismiss Marnie. Marnie felt trapped by the penetrating gaze of his eyes as she stared up at him, wondering as she did how the whole situation could have gone so hopelessly wrong.

But if he was going to dismiss her he was certainly in no hurry to do so. His eyes remained on her face and Marnie realised with a sinking heart that he was enjoying, actually enjoying, torturing her.

'I like the idea of a tree and a turkey,' he said at last, his teeth flashing white against the dark hue of his skin. Marnie held her breath waiting for him to continue. 'We'll have *our* Christmas dinner at seven.' His smile deepened and Marnie's heart beat wildly against her ribs. 'Do you think you could look after the details?'

Marnie nodded and swallowed hard. 'Yes, I would like to do that,' she agreed a little breathlessly. 'Eva and I will go tomorrow and pick out a tree. We can decorate it Christmas Eve and I know the best place to get a turkey and . . .'

'*Eva!?*' Helena's voice was a loud screech. 'Did you hear that, Conrad? She called your grandmother *Eva!*'

'Well that is my name, after all,' Eva piped up.

Helena glared down at her and snatched her arms from Eva's shoulders. She marched over to stand beside Conrad. 'How much more of this disrespect are you going to allow?' Helena demanded to know.

Conrad shrugged his broad shoulders and Marnie saw the muscles tighten under his shirt, only this time she knew his annoyance was directed at Helena and not at herself for once.

'If Eva,' and here he turned to his grandmother and smiled at her, 'wants Marnie to call her by her Christian name then it's certainly all right by me. Besides,' he added as an afterthought, 'it's rather nice to hear you called by that again.' He reached over and covered his grandmother's hand. 'Eva,' he said softly. Eva placed her other hand on top of his, and there were tears in her eyes. It was a tender, sensitive moment and it was a moment which belonged to them. Unfortunately, Helena didn't see it that way, if she saw it at all.

'Well I for one respect my elders and wouldn't dream of calling *an old lady* by her first name!' she huffed angrily, returning to her chair as Flora and Annie brought in the dessert. Did Marnie imagine it or did a conspiratorial look pass between Helena and Flora? But whatever it was it was gone before Marnie could properly analyse it. The dessert was passed around, thick wedges of a pavlova made with swirls of cream and tropical fruits.

The dessert was over and coffee was being served when Helena said, 'I'll look after the Christmas dinner, Conrad. I'll get the tree and the turkey if that's what you insist on, but I don't feel there is any need to keep Marnie here over Christmas. After all,' she smiled sweetly at Marnie, 'you will want to be with your own family.'

Conrad put down his cup and studied Marnie. 'But of course,' he agreed slowly, but Marnie got the distinct impression that he wanted her to stay. His eyes held a question and she knew what her answer would be. She turned to Helena and returned Helena's sweet smile.

'My parents are holidaying in Africa and my aunt and uncle already know that if the arrangements here didn't fit in with their plans then not to expect me for dinner.' She returned her glance to Conrad. 'I'll be happy to attend to all the details just as you asked me.'

'Good. It's settled then.' He looked relieved but there was something else. Marnie caught the look in his eye and a smile hovered on her lips. For once he had taken her side against Helena and although this was a small victory it made her feel all warm inside.

He turned to Helena. 'You will be busy enough with our guests without tiring yourself in the kitchen!'

'But of course, darling,' Helena simpered, flashing a triumphant glance at Marnie. 'I was just thinking about Marnie that's all.'

'And I'm sure she appreciates your concern,' he answered mildly, his black eyes settling on Marnie's flushed features as though he expected her to thank Helena for her generosity.

'Yes ... yes, Helena,' Marnie mumbled and then summoning all the will-power she possessed managed to look Helena straight in the eye. 'You enjoy your guests and try not to worry about me!'

Helena's green eyes narrowed at this and Marnie actually felt the hairs on her neck stand on end at the naked cruelty in Helena's eyes. Helena said: 'I won't. Not with Flora and Annie helping you in the kitchen!' A sliver of a smile snaked along her heavily rouged lips before she turned from Marnie to look at Conrad. 'And of course I will enjoy *our* guests,' she gushed.

But Conrad's mind was obviously on other business now that the tree and the turkey had been dispensed with. He drained the last of his coffee from the cup and set it firmly down on the saucer, twisting his wrist to glance at his watch, a gesture Marnie was becoming quite familiar with.

'I'm expecting an important telephone call in a few minutes,' he said, rising to his feet. 'If anyone needs me I'll be in my study for the rest of the evening.'

And then he was gone, his long legs carrying him with the easy grace of an athlete as he made his way to his study. Marnie sighed as she watched him go. It didn't seem fair that one man should have to work so hard and have such long hours.

'Well, that leaves me with nothing to do the whole night,' Helena grumbled, throwing her napkin on to the table. She yawned and stretched and looked across at Eva. 'You should take your meals upstairs in your room,' she snapped. 'After all that is why you had Conrad install that kitchen for you.'

'Marnie doesn't like me eating upstairs,' Eva replied nervously. 'Marnie thinks I was spending too much of my time alone.'

Helena's icy green eyes flashed briefly at Marnie. 'Of course Marnie would say that,' she sneered. 'If you ate upstairs then she would have to eat upstairs too. Then she wouldn't have Conrad to moon over at the table.' The icy green eyes returned once more to Marnie. 'But I think Conrad has shown you just what he thinks of you. He sees you as a maid . . . a cook!' Helena laughed softly. 'While you spend Christmas day cooking *our* dinner Conrad and I and our guests will be frolicking around the pool.' She rose from the table, a vision in shimmering gold. 'Well, you take care of *Eva*,' she said to Marnie, 'and I will go upstairs to my room and do my hair and nails.'

Before Marnie or Eva had a chance to reply Helena was gone, only the scent of her perfume lingering in the dining room.

'Is she always that rude?' Marnie gasped in amazement, her eyes fixed on the door Helena had just passed through.

'She's always been a little, well hard, if you know what I mean,' Eva sighed. 'She comes every holiday so I guess I'm quite used to her.'

Marnie's mouth tightened as she looked at Eva. Eva was hardly a fair match for Helena's particular brand of hardness.

'There's never any excuse for rudeness,' Marnie said as she sipped slowly at her cold coffee.

'I think something is bothering her,' Eva replied in Helena's defence. 'I think it has something to do with you. I get the feeling she doesn't like you being here. Now isn't that silly?'

'Very!' Marnie replied grimly.

Later that evening Marnie stood on the balcony off her bedroom. She had bathed and was wearing only a thin cotton nightie allowing the cool sea breezes to temper down the heat of her body. Across the sweeping lawns flooded in moonlight she could see the silvery stretch of beach flanked on one side with gracefully swaying palms and on the other by the whispering foaming surge of the sea. She placed her hands on the railing and leaned forward, hoping the thrusting sounds of the waves would drown out Helena's hateful words.

But the waves only seemed to pound them further into her brain and she took her hands from the rail to press her fingers against her aching temples. Helena had been nasty to Eva and that in itself was unforgivable but it was the words she had flung at Marnie which were causing her so much grief. *He sees you as a maid . . . a cook!* The words resounded in her ears over and over again as the waves pounded them home.

Marnie left the rail and leaned against the sandstone brick, her arms held behind her, feeling the heat of the wall which had basked all day in the sun. Her head was tilted back and her large blue eyes gazed up at the sparkling diamonds splattered in organised fashion across the velvet blackness of the clear, coastal sky. The moon was full. A giant orb leading the stars to flood the earth below.

And to shine on the glistening tears which sparkled on Marnie's silky lashes. Impatiently she brushed them away and stepped back into her room. She had been so eager to volunteer her services she thought ruefully and had even been thrilled when Conrad handed the responsibility of the Christmas dinner over to her. She had thought it was his way of proving to her that he had faith and trust in her, that he was in fact offering her an olive branch. But instead he had merely handed her these duties so Helena would be spared from them. In his eyes she was an employee, it was as simple as that. A maid, a cook, a companion. That's how he saw her and she was a fool if she expected anything else.

Marnie strolled restlessly about her room, picking up articles and putting them down again. It was late, the house had long been quiet and she knew she was the only one not to be in bed. But if she tried to sleep now she would end up tossing and turning and not being able to get any sleep at all. She impulsively opened her bedroom door and peered down the hall. All was quiet. Moonlight filtered through the end windows lighting up the passageway. She stepped out into the hall and closed her door behind her. Within minutes she was flying across the landscaped gardens making her way to the beach.

She stood at the water's edge delighting in the soft warm foam tugging gently at her toes. Her feet sank into the sand as the ever-heaving waters pulled the minute granules from under her. She felt free here. The summer breeze filtered her thoughts, cleansing them, and gradually the sting of Helena's words lost their sharpness. Only the knowledge that Conrad would never look past the point where he saw her as just another of his employees left her with a deep aching throb in the vicinity of her heart.

'Marnie!'

Marnie whirled around to see Conrad standing directly behind her. His black hair fell over his forehead mussed from sleep or wind. He was wearing a black silk robe and it hung loose as though he had put in on in a hurry and hadn't bothered to tie it around his waist. His chest was bare. She could see the fine black hairs veeing down to the waistband of the boxer-type shorty pyjamas men wear in warm climates.

He reached out and smoothed her hair away from her cheeks and smiled down at her when the wind tossed it back again.

'Couldn't you sleep?' he asked softly.

'Couldn't you?' Marnie asked, returning his question.

A low chuckle escaped from the strong brown column of his throat. 'I haven't been to bed,' he told her, reaching out again to tuck her hair behind her ears, only this time his hands remained to cradle her face between them. 'I had just finished having a shower and turned out my light when I saw a tiny elf dressed in white floating across the lawn and down to the beach. I decided I had better investigate.'

Marnie reached up to take his hands from her face but instead of tugging at his fingers as she had intended to do, she found herself holding on to them. Her short cotton nightie whipped around her slender legs and she could feel his bare legs against the bareness of her own. A spasm of excitement shook her and she shivered, her whole body trembling at being so close to his own.

His smile disappeared and a dark intensity shone from his eyes as he searched her face. His hands moved down to lightly circle her neck and then to rest on her bare shoulders. Her own hands were still on his, her beautiful eyes misty with the emotions which were raging within her.

She felt herself being drawn closer to the hard, lean

length of his body, and his hands tightened on her shoulders. The moonlight bathed them in splendour and stars were reflected in their eyes. He lowered his head and briefly touched her lips with his. Marnie's hands were now on his chest, the palms flattened against the silky hairs. She stared up at him, her lips burning from the touch of his mouth. With a strangled cry he crushed her to him and he was kissing her hungrily, his mouth bruising and demanding as he explored the sweet interior of her petal-soft mouth.

Her arms moved up and her fingers were running through the thick luxurious mass of his hair. She was aware of her body pressing against his, of his hands moulding her slender frame into the rugged hardness of his own. The waves seemed to wash over them, giving Marnie the sensation of drowning and she clung to him the way she had in the surf.

His flesh seared her own, the cotton nightie offering her no protection against his potent male virility. Her bare feet sank deeper into the soft sand, the tide water licking at her ankles. She felt weightless as though her body had somehow flowed into his. His mouth left hers to trace a burning trail across to her ear and then down the slender column of her neck.

Marnie arched against him, completely lost now, abandoning herself to his wild seductive embraces. He slipped the tiny straps of her nightie from her shoulders, exposing the creamy smoothness of rounded breasts. He lifted her against him, crushing their fullness against his massive chest and then she was lying beside him, cradled in his arms. His fingers gently stroked the curve of her cheek, passing down her neck and finally cupping her breast, his thumb caressing the erected peak. Marnie moaned as every nerve in her body cried out for release from this exquisitely delicious agony.

His lips were carrying out their own particular brand

of seduction, nuzzling and nibbling and finally claiming her breast as his mouth closed over the throbbing, swollen bud. She felt his hand on her thigh as he pulled up the flimsy scrap of material, his fingers moving dangerously close to that part of her which she had always vowed would be reserved for the man she eventually married. Marnie stirred against him, her movements becoming frantic as she fought against the magic of his touch.

He leaned over her, murmuring against the pulse beating frantically in the hollow of her neck. 'Marnie . . . God . . .! Don't fight me!'

Sanity returned to her as she felt him pressing against her thighs. 'No!' she gasped, her hands leaving the thick scrub of his hair to push against his chest. 'I can't! No, please don't!'

He stiffened against her, supporting the bulk of his weight with his arms as he leaned over her. Her eyes were wide with passion and fear as she gazed helplessly up at him. The moon shone fully on her face, highlighting the delicate structure of her features, the softness of trembling lips. His own face was in shadows, his eyes hooded as he bent over her. A gleam of white flashed briefly as a savage oath tore from his lips and then he was gone, his legs drawn up as he sat beside her.

Marnie hardly dared breathe. She lay like a statue staring up at the sky, conscious only of his anger and the still frantic beating of her heart. She felt rather than saw him turn towards her, his hands surprisingly gentle as he pulled down the skirt of her nightie and pulled up the top to cover her breasts. With her modesty reasonably restored she felt confident enough to look at him. He was looking out over the waters, his profile rigid, as if it had been carved from stone. She longed to touch him, to place her hand against his cheek. Instead, she clutched at the material of her nightie, her hand falling down to feel the smoothness of silk. It was only then she realised he had removed his robe and she was lying on it. When had he done it, she wondered now, her eyes travelling across the velvet smoothness of his naked shoulders. It had all happened so quickly. One minute she had been standing in front of him, the next she had been in his arms. Like the force of the moon upon the tides his sheer magnetism had drawn her to him.

Marnie pulled herself into a sitting position, careful not to touch the broad shoulder which was so perilously close to her own small one. She drew her knees up to her chest and pulled her nightie over them, resting her chin on her arms as she folded them across her knees. The waves lapped against the shore, a curiously soothing sound, and the soft summer breeze gently fanned them. The waters sparkled and shimmered under the moonlit sky, the waves tumbling and churning like effervescent vollup cascading and disappearing finally into a waterbed of stardust.

Conrad turned towards her and she felt his eyes on her face. Slowly she turned to him, her head tilted to look into his strong features.

'Why did you come down here?' he asked in a choking voice.

Marnie took a deep breath before answering. 'It was as you said earlier,' she confessed. 'I couldn't sleep, or at least I thought I wouldn't be able to sleep.'

His eyes were still on her and she met his gaze unflinchingly. He seemed to be examining her features in great detail and to her amazement she found she was doing the same. Funny how she had never noticed how deep the cleft in his chin was, she thought now, and the tips of her fingers ached to touch it, to explore the strong line of his jaw, to feel the stubble of his whiskers, which she knew would be shaved off come morning.

He was looking at her mouth and she looked at his, thrilling at the memory of those hard lips on hers, of that handsome full mouth exploring, touching, tasting ...! She tore her eyes away before he had a chance to guess at her thoughts. Her mouth felt suddenly dry as she stared out again at the throbbing waters.

'You weren't worried about the Christmas dinner were you?' he asked and Marnie's head swung around, her large violet-blue eyes puzzled for a moment and then clearing. She smiled more at herself than at him. She had quite forgotten the Christmas dinner. And then memory claimed her in an almost paralysing grip.

The Christmas dinner *and* Helena! Good grief, how could she have forgotten the reason, the *real* reason why she had fled her room to find sanctuary at the beach. *He sees you as a maid ... a cook!* Helena's cruel barbs came back to haunt her and with a strangled cry Marnie stumbled to her feet, her face pale and her eyes huge and appearing black in the pale oval of her face as she stared down at his astonished features. Her small hands were clenched into fists at her sides as she fought back the tears which were threatening to expose her. How would he see her now she wondered brokenly, as visions of their lovemaking came back to her. It had been so beautiful. But now ... now she saw it as Helena would, how Conrad most probably had. A cheap fling in the sand.

He sprang easily to his feet, picking up his robe as he did so and draping it across her shoulders. She huddled into it, thankful not for the warmth because she wasn't cold, but it hid her from him and this now seemed very important. He placed a finger under her **chin** and made her look at him.

'You *are* worried about the dinner.' He smiled down into her sad little face, 'you needn't be. Flora and Annie will do most of the work. You will be the overseer.' His smile deepened and she forced herself to smile back. He wasn't aware of the torment in her heart and she knew he must never know, never guess or suspect that what had been a cheap fling for him had been the most beautiful experience in her life.

He put his arm around her shoulders and guided her back to the house. She could never remember afterwards what they had talked about. She could only remember how miserable she had felt while she had listened to the sound of his deeply timbred voice.

And to the sound of her heart as it beat out the rhythm of love. She had fallen hopelessly in love with a man she knew she could never have.

CHAPTER SIX

THE toast had just popped out of the toaster when Conrad entered the kitchen. Marnie was shocked by his appearance. He was dressed, but he hadn't shaved and weary lines were etched around his eyes. It was obvious he hadn't been to bed the night before.

He took a tall glass from one of the cupboards and walked over to the two-door fridge-freezer combination and poured himself a glass of orange juice. Marnie spread butter and jam on the toast, aware of his eyes watching her as she cut the toast into squares and placed them on to a plate. Next she poured some coffee into a cup and placed the coffee along with the plate of toast on to the kitchen table. He was still watching her, his ankles crossed as he leaned against the fridge.

'Sit down and eat,' she quietly ordered him, indicating the food on the table. 'I'll make you some bacon and eggs.'

She turned to get a pan from the cupboard but he surprised her by grabbing her wrist. 'Marnie, we've got to talk.'

'Wh-What about?' she asked weakly, knowing full well it would be about last night.

A faint smile threw some relief into his grimly dark features. 'I think you already know.' He released her wrist and put his glass of juice down on the table, shoving both his hands into his jeans pockets.

'Last night,' he began slowly, his eyes meeting hers, 'was something which shouldn't have happened.' He sucked in his breath and drew out his hands, spreading them in a hopeless gesture. 'It was my fault. I was

96

strictly out of line. I'd like you to know that it won't happen again.'

Hot colour seared Marnie's cheeks. So it had meant nothing to him. Their lovemaking had been something which shouldn't have happened and he was warning her not to read anything important into it. She swallowed the lump in her throat and bravely looked up at him.

'Oh,' she said. 'You mean down on the beach. I'd already forgotten about *that*!' Her laugh was shaky. 'Good heavens, Conrad, surely you didn't waste any sleep worrying if I had fallen in love with you over a few silly kisses?' She laughed again and pulled a pan from the cupboard. 'Men!' she exclaimed, peeping at him sideways. 'You're such a conceited lot!'

Her back was facing him as she turned to the stove, frantically blinking back her tears. Her heart felt like every last drop of blood had been painfully wrung from it.

'I can see I worried about nothing,' he growled behind her and she heard and was puzzled by the anger in his voice, when there should only have been relief. 'Had I thought you considered my lovemaking "silly" I wouldn't have allowed you to get off so easily. I thought I was saving your virtue, but I can see now I only prevented myself from becoming an even bigger fool than I already consider myself.'

She whirled to face him, bacon in her hands. 'Then you should be thanking me instead of apologising to me.' she flared. 'And to spare you any further grief let me tell you I'm perfectly aware of my position here.'

His brows knitted together in a frown. 'Your position? he queried. 'What's that supposed to mean?'

She turned back to the stove, chewing on her bottom lip. 'Never mind,' she mumbled, wishing now she hadn't pursued this discussion. She should have let him say his piece, agreed with him and let the matter drop. He came up behind her and turned her around. She held the packet of bacon between them, thinking it would offer some protection, some insulation for her senses.

'I asked you a question Marnie and I expect an answer.' His hands tightened on her shoulders and his eyes searched hers.

'I was just being foolish,' she answered glibly and even managed a small shrug. 'I am an employee of yours and I'm willing to accept any rules laid down by you. If you say no more fun and games on the beach then that's fine by me.'

Her eyes were unnaturally bright as she gazed up at him, and his own eyes were hard and cold as he glared down into her upturned face. His fingers bit into her shoulders and then he took his hands away, letting them fall to his sides. 'Just as long as we understand each other,' he returned savagely, 'then *that*'s also fine with me!'

She thought he would leave, but to her astonishment he sat down at the table and looked expectantly up at her. 'Well? Stop standing there staring at me and get me some breakfast.'

Marnie's cheeks fused with colour, but she turned back to the stove and started putting strips of bacon into the pan. She had made the initial offer of cooking him breakfast but as she cracked eggs into the pan she couldn't help think that indeed he did see her as a cook!

His eyes followed her every move as she darted about the enormous kitchen getting things for his breakfast. She wondered what Flora and Annie would think if they happened to come into the kitchen now and see her preparing Conrad's breakfast. But a surreptitious glance at her watch told her it would be at least another half hour before either woman put in an appearance; for then it was still early, not yet six o'clock.

'Aren't you having any?' he asked as she set his

plate down in front of him.

Marnie looked at the toast she had offered him earlier and which he hadn't eaten. 'I'll take this back,' she said, picking up the plate and carrying it over to the counter. She picked up one of the squares and began nibbling on it. It tasted awful.

He picked up knife and fork and began eating. 'No wonder you're so small if that's an example of what you usually eat for breakfast,' he admonished her, his eyes trailing over her slender figure.

'I haven't got time to eat much this morning,' she answered, marvelling at their casual conversation.

'Oh? Why's that?'

'The tree, remember. I'm getting it this morning.'

'Ah, yes, the tree.' He finished the last of his bacon and egg. 'That was very nice.' He smiled at her. 'I can't remember the last time I ate in the kitchen.' He pushed himself away from the table, tilting his chair back. She noticed he didn't look nearly so tired. 'I'll go with you to get the tree.'

This unexpected bit of news filled her with pleasure, and she didn't have a chance to mask her happiness from her eyes before he had seen it. Amusement flashed briefly in his coal black eyes. He got up from his chair and stood in front of her, his finger hooking her chin. 'Would you like me to go with you?' he asked wickedly, and there was nothing for Marnie to do but nod her head in agreement because she had already given herself away.

'Good,' he said softly, his thumb moving up to stroke her cheek. Marnie's heart was thumping so loudly she was terrified he might hear it and draw his own conclusions. 'We can get a nice one in Manly. I know a guy who sells them.'

His hand was cupping the side of her face now, the base of his palm lifting her chin. Marnie felt her lips parting as he slowly lowered his head. His mouth covered hers and she felt his hand on her back pressing her against him. Every nerve in her body responded to his kiss and her veins became a network of flames. Her lips clung to his, reluctant to let the kiss end. He smiled down at her, triumph gleaming in his eyes.

'Another silly kiss to add to your collection, mmm?' he taunted her softly, his mouth hovering above hers, inviting her to kiss him back. His hand left her face to join his other behind her back, holding her in a tight embrace.

Her body betrayed her. It responded to his with a will of its own. She felt her arms moving slowly upwards, her fingers in his hair. His eyes held hers in an hypnotic embrace and she stood on her tiptoes to press her mouth against his. His hands moved down to her hips, moulding her against him, making her thrillingly aware of his male hardness.

Her mouth had been gentle on his own, a shy almost timid gesture, but one she had been quite willing to make.

'Come on, Marnie,' he whispered against her lips. 'You can do better than that!'

Sanity returned to her and with it a wild hatred for what he was doing to her. She realised she had hurt his male ego by referring to his lovemaking as 'silly' and now he was intent on punishing her by robbing her of her own pride. It wasn't enough that he had practically made her beg for his kisses, but now he was trying to make it seem as though *she* was the one seducing *him*!

Her hands grabbed his hair and she pulled on it . . .*hard*! She had the satisfaction of seeing his eyes widen in surprise and she even smiled when she saw him wince. But her smile froze on her face when she saw the enraged look which flared in his eyes. His hands whipped up to her own hair and she gave a small gasp as she was forced to look into the glittering blackness of a devil's eyes. His face was flushed with rage and the handsome line of his mouth was pulled back in a snarl. Marnie stared at him, certain he was going to murder her.

His eyes held hers in a searing embrace and then with a strangled cry his mouth covered hers in a bruising kiss. When it was over Marnie could taste blood in her mouth. He set her away from him and he stood watching her, his shoulders hunched and his lips pressed together.

Marnie was completely shaken and her knees were wobbling. She reached for a chair and held on to it for support, her eyes not daring to leave his face in case he attacked her again. She expected an apology and waited to receive it, determined she wouldn't forgive him for his brutal behaviour. When it became obvious that none would be forthcoming she put a hand up to her mouth.

'You hurt me,' she accused him in a hurt, angry voice.

'You deserved it,' he flung back without remorse.

She smoothed her pink jersey, tucking the waistband into her white slacks. Her hands were trembling as she flicked her hair behind her ears. 'You said ...' She swallowed hard and tried again, a tremor in her voice, 'You said you stepped out of line last night and that ... nothing like it would happen again.'

Her violet eyes were stormy as she glared across at him, wondering what his reaction would be at having his own words flung back at him. He squared his shoulders, muscles rippling under the navy T-shirt he was wearing. An easy smile spread slowly across his craggy features throwing them into light relief.

'That's right,' he drawled. 'Last night I did step out of line, but not this morning. This morning you received exactly what you deserved. Now if you're ready to get that tree I suggest we go. I don't want Helena to have to receive our visitors on her own.'

He carried his dishes over to the sink and rinsed them, quite as though nothing important had transpired between them. Marnie remained standing by the chair, trying to gather her composure. When he turned back to her she hoped she appeared calmer than she felt.

'Ready?' he asked.

'I hadn't intended to go this early,' she told him stiffly.

'Perhaps not, but this is the only time *I* can go.' he answered impatiently.

'I had planned to take Eva with me. She won't be up for another hour or so. Then there's her breakfast and . . .'

'Flora can make her breakfast,' he interrupted. 'Now if there aren't any further excuses perhaps we can get a move on.' He glanced at his watch and frowned.

'For heaven's sake, Conrad, if you're in that much of a hurry why bother coming at all? I don't need you to help pick out a tree and I don't feel like being rushed.'

'You do need me,' he rounded on her harshly. 'How do you propose to get the tree home? It certainly won't fit in the boot of your car.'

'Well . . . well, I could probably have it delivered.' But even as she said this Marnie knew it was most unlikely she would find anyone willing to deliver a Christmas tree so far up the coast. Conrad merely raised his brows in an arrogant fashion and managed to look suitably exasperated. He reached for her hand and led her to the door.

'Come on, Marnie, we'll take my ute.' He opened the door and she stepped through into the bright morning sunshine. As she followed him to the garage she looked up at Eva's bedroom window. A worried frown crossed her brow. She stopped and wrung her hands. She couldn't . . . just couldn't go and leave Eva alone even if it was just for an hour. Not with Flora and Annie in attendance. Not with Helena there, with her cutting and cruel barbs.

'For God's sake Marnie! What is it now?'

'I don't feel right about leaving Eva.'

Conrad took her arm and steered her to the ute. 'Eva's been left alone before and survived,' he told her with a smile. 'She's not a baby you know and I don't think she would appreciate having you think and treat her as one.' He opened the door of the ute and helped Marnie inside, firmly closing the door against any further protests.

The drive down the coastal road was extremely enjoyable. Marnie got the distinct impression that Conrad was enjoying the freedom of getting away from the house and, in particular, the telephone. Several times Marnie glanced at him and each time he appeared to be more relaxed. The traffic was light, the scenery beautiful, with emerald green waters and cloudless blue skies sweeping beside and above them. The fresh salt air was invigorating, the slight breeze sweeping Marnie's hair around her face.

She thought of Eva. Eva had been tired the night before and perhaps she would still be sleeping when they got back. Still, Marnie couldn't help but feel worried and guilty about leaving the house without Eva knowing. It just didn't seem right and she cast Conrad a scornful glance. He had bullied her into leaving before she was ready, just like he had bullied her about everything else.

But on such a fine day one couldn't stay cross or worried for long. By the time they got to Manly the fresh air, the sunshine, the white sands and the foamy surfing beaches had all contributed to making Marnie feel wonderfully and gloriously alive. If the man with his windswept hair and unshaven face had anything to do with her feeling of well-being, Marnie wasn't prepared to say. All she knew was that she was glad (just this once) that he had bullied her into coming, early or not.

They drove along the esplanade beside the harbour. Already families had congregated on the beach, while others were strolling along the boardwalk. Loud screeching parrots flew above the pine trees and seagulls circled around couples on benches, hoping for a tid-bit or two. Conrad drove slowly along, turning left on to the Corso which stretched between the harbour and Manly's famous surfing beach. Sunlight sparkled on the rolling waters and brightly coloured umbrellas were being erected on the white sands.

The Manly Surf Life Saving Club were practising safety patrols on the beach while their boat squads were perfecting manoeuvres in the wild surf. Conrad followed the ocean road, stopping at a small greengrocers which was just opening. The owner of the shop greeted Conrad with a wild shout and a delighted grin spread across his face. Conrad jumped down from the ute and gave the short, rough-looking man a hug. Both men stood back and joked with one another, breaking into wild shouts of laughter while Marnie sat in the ute looking on in amazement. She couldn't believe Conrad could be so totally relaxed, so *human*!

Finally he turned back to the ute and opened the door, helping Marnie out. He introduced her to his friend and the man's dark eyes twinkled. He gave Conrad a conspiratorial wink as he openly appraised her, his eyes reflecting his appreciation of Marnie's slender build and delicate beauty. Marnie flushed and ignored the jab Conrad's friend gave to his arm.

With the 'preliminaries' over, the two men got down to business, Conrad explaining about the type of tree they wanted and the man insisting he had just the one. He led them around to the back of the shop where only a few trees remained. None of them were suitable Marnie saw at a glance.

However, Conrad apparently thought them just fine. The only difficulty, he was explaining to his friend, was which one to take. He turned to Marnie.

'You choose,' he said.

Both men watched her while she watched the trees. They were so thin and sparse that she felt sure they would be blown away with each small gust of wind. She shook her head.

'I don't think . . .' she began, but Conrad cut in.

'This one,' he decided, reaching for and picking up one of the trees. He turned to his friend. 'How much do I owe you, Rudy?'

Rudy laughed. 'Not a cent. It's Christmas, let it be a gift, old friend.'

The tree was placed in the back of the ute and after a few more guffaws, Conrad finally got in and off they drove.

'Cheer up,' he chuckled after a few moments, 'it will look great once it's decorated.'

Marnie looked across at him and had to smile. He looked so relaxed, so charmingly boyish in his carefree mood that she found she didn't want to do anything which might spoil his present good humour.

'Do you have enough decorations at home?' she asked. 'Or should we buy some?'

'There's a box filled with the things in the basement,' he told her with great gusto. 'They haven't been brought out in years. I think the last time we had a proper tree was when I was fifteen or sixteen.' He shook his head. 'Time flies, doesn't it?' He didn't wait for an answer, his eyes glued to the ever-increasing traffic as he manoeuvred the ute between cars and pedestrians.

'Of course,' he continued in his relaxed, easy tones, 'we've always had some sort of tree. One of those small artificial ones which sit on the dining room table. Pretty enough but not like the real thing, wouldn't you say?'

Marnie opened her mouth to respond, but he rushed on and she knew he was deliberately not giving her an opportunity to speak. Not that she minded. She was enjoying listening to him.

'Grandmother will get the biggest kick out of the tree,' he assured her, turning to give Marnie a disarming smile which left no doubt in Marnie's mind that he was the one looking forward to the tree and that in comparison anybody else's enjoyment would be half-hearted to say the least. A smile hovered on her lips, and she relaxed into her seat. She had a feeling it was going to be a great Christmas.

Conrad parked the ute in front of a butcher's shop. 'Now for old Tom Turkey, eh?' he said, as he turned off the motor.

Conrad was on the same friendly terms with the butcher as he had been with the greengrocer. After their initial boisterous greeting Conrad got down to business. By the time they left the shop he was wielding a huge box containing two large turkeys and an enormous leg of ham. The box was placed beside the tree in the back of the ute and when they got in and drove off Marnie wasn't in the least surprised to hear Conrad say: 'I can almost taste that turkey now!' He added anxiously. 'How are you at making dressing?'

'Pretty good,' she admitted with a chuckle.

'And gravy?'

'Without lumps,' she assured him happily.

'I can't believe it,' he pretended to sigh. 'Beauty, brains and gravy without lumps! It's truly a miracle some man hasn't grabbed you and married you!'

'I know,' she returned his sigh, 'but then not many men know about the gravy!'

He laughed and looked across at her, his eyes warm on her face. Marnie turned away, her heart throbbing against her ribs. He reached over and grabbed her hand, giving it a squeeze before placing it to his lips. She jerked her hand away and folded both hands in her lap.

'What's wrong?' he drawled, his tone innocent.

Marnie shrugged one dainty shoulder. 'Just remembering your advice back at the house,' she replied with dignity, not looking at him. 'I don't want you blaming me every time you step out of line!'

His easy laughter flowed over her, warming her in a cloak of velvet and bringing a hot flush to her cheeks. A reluctant smile tugged at the corners of her mouth as her eyes were drawn to his and she felt a thrill of excitement race up and down her spine. Even when he had turned his attention back to the traffic she found she couldn't tear her eyes away from his profile.

He stopped the ute again, this time in front of a Tea Shoppe. Marnie looked at him questioningly. He flashed her a mischievous glance. 'Time to eat. You look hungry and that bit of toast you had for breakfast couldn't still be with you. Besides,' he said as he helped her down from the ute, 'they make the best scones here of any place I know.'

The Tea Shoppe was designed like a cosy kitchen and the woman who ran it was plump and jolly. It didn't surprise Marnie in the least that Conrad was on a first-name basis with the owner of the shop, who greeted him like a long lost son. Several minutes were spent on catching up with the news and then the woman escorted them out to a small tiled balcony overlooking the harbour. Conrad ordered tea and scones with fresh strawberry jam and cream.

Below them on the rocks stood several men and a few boys with fishing rods in their hands. The waves washed over their feet and some of them came dangerously close to being swept off the huge jutting rocks. Further out the Manly Ferry was chugging its way to the wharf to pick up the waiting passengers and carry them back to Sydney. Hydrofoils skimmed over the sparkling waters, and several sailing craft were being prepared for a race. The soft breeze was warm and gentle and added to Marnie's appetite. She ate heartily of the delicious featherlight scones topped with jam and plenty of cream and washed them down with several cups of steaming hot tea.

Their conversation was light and casual and extremely enjoyable, with each telling the other about family customs and traditions at Christmas and Marnie had to laugh when Conrad said the best tradition was the turkey with all the trimmings.

'How can you even think about food after what you've just eaten?' she admonished him good-naturedly. 'I was counting you know, and you devoured no less than eight scones.'

'You mean I ate most of them?' he asked in mock horror. 'I thought you cleaned the plate.'

'No, but I think I'm guilty about eating most of the cream,' she confessed with a groan, but nevertheless couldn't resist putting in a pink fingertip and scooping out the last little bit of cream. She licked the cream from her finger and leaned back in her white wicker chair, her large violet eyes wandering over to the clump of sweet smelling frangipani trees with their creamy white blossoms and pale yellow centres. Overhead, brilliant red bougainvillaea wound its way through the pergola which sheltered them from the hot sun.

She watched Conrad stretch back in his chair, totally relaxed for once, his eyes closed, his long lashes lying against his cheeks gave him an innocent and vulnerable appearance. Good thing she knew better, she found herself thinking ruefully. His eyes flew open and there was a glint of humour in their sparkling depths, making her wonder if he had heard her thoughts.

'We had better be going,' she murmured softly and he smiled at the reluctance in her voice.

He pulled himself up in his chair and then stood, lifting his arms as he stretched. 'Too many of those,' he growled, indicating the empty scone plate, 'and I wouldn't be fit for much.' He reached for her hand and pulled her from her chair, drawing her close against his chest. Her breath caught in her throat as his eyes held hers in a seductive embrace.

With great difficulty she managed to drag her eyes away, concentrating on the stitching surrounding the neck of his shirt.

'Your grandmother will be up by now,' she husked softly, 'and she'll be wondering where I am.' Helena's image flashed in front of her eyes. '*Everyone* will be wondering where we are,' she added on a worried note.

'Well, when we arrive with the tree and the turkey and the ham they'll know where we've been and,' he hugged her, 'what we've been doing!'

Marnie pushed herself away, knowing he was deliberately teasing her. She could still feel his arms around her long after they had settled themselves in the ute and were on the coastal road home. It was still early, but she couldn't help the pangs of guilt which consistently washed over her whenever she thought of leaving Eva alone. Pangs of guilt which seemed even worse because she had enjoyed herself so much. Conrad was quiet on the way back and she found herself wondering if perhaps he didn't feel a little guilty himself. She saw him glance at his watch and she hugged the sides of her seat as he increased the ute's speed.

'We haven't been gone too long,' she yelled at him over the wind pouring into the vehicle.

He wound up his window and she followed suit by winding up her own. The silence was immediate.

'No, but I've got to shave and light the barbecue,' he informed her impatiently, his easy comraderie completely gone. 'Helena thought it would be a good idea to welcome our guests with steaks and salad.'

'Oh,' Marnie replied on a dull note. It seemed he was driving even faster. Was his need to get to Helena and cater to her whims so great that he would risk having an accident? Her eyes crept nervously to the speedometer and widened in horror.

'Slow down!' she begged, clutching at his arm. He half turned towards her and then he glanced at the speedometer. To her relief he dropped his speed and she took her hand away.

'Sorry,' he muttered, and then, 'Did I frighten you?'

'Not me,' she returned breathlessly, 'but you gave the birds a fright! They must have thought there was a wingless wonder introduced to the area.'

The remark was meant for humour but he didn't laugh. Not that she expected him to she thought dismally, when he had other more important things on his mind . . . like Helena and his guests and the barbecue! Still she thought, it would be good for him to relax with his friends and get away from the pressures of his business for a while. She wondered how many days he would take off, but one glance at his stony profile made her guess it wouldn't be too many. Was it the money he was after she wondered or was it the driving need to restore what his father had lost? Was it his reputation as a shrewd and successful business man which drove him, or was it the desire to prove to the world that the Wrights' were alive and well and making it in Sydney?

They were on the almost deserted stretch of road

which led to the house. Conrad slowed the ute to almost a crawl. Marnie leaned forward, her small perfect teeth clenched on her bottom lip. Her eyes were troubled as she gave him a hasty glance.

'Oh, I do hope Eva is all right,' she said in a small, worried voice. Her hands were clenched in a tight ball on her lap.

His eyes narrowed shrewdly on her face. 'Why wouldn't she be all right?' He turned his attention back to the road and swung into the long driveway leading to the house. 'There's three women to look after her. You make grandmother sound like a cantankerous juvenile instead of a grown woman!'

Marnie shifted in her seat. 'It's just that she's so small and helpless against . . .'

He turned on her angrily. 'For God's sake, Marnie,' he snapped. 'Surely you're not still insinuating that my grandmother is at some sort of risk in her own home?'

For answer Marnie closed her eyes and leaned back against the head rest.

'I've questioned Grandmother,' he went on in a tight voice, 'and she has assured me that everything is fine. I've even discussed the matter with Helena and she thought your ideas were quite extraordinary to say the least! Now for all our sakes, would you please let the matter drop so we can have a peaceful Christmas. It is, after all, for Eva that we're doing all this . . . the turkey and the tree.'

'I thought our discussions concerning your grand-mother were private,' Marnie fumed. 'I didn't expect you to go behind my back and talk to Helena about it.'

'Why shouldn't I? Helena is a friend, a close friend of the family. At first she was very concerned when I told her what your observations were and then we both agreed you were barking up the wrong tree. There's nothing wrong in my house, I can assure you!'

'Considering it was Helena who found Flora and Annie for you I'm not at all surprised that she would defend them. Has she ever told you *where* she found them?'

'As a matter of fact she did. They used to work for friends of her parents. They moved to Europe. Helena knew of my situation here and on my behalf put the positions to Flora and Annie and they readily accepted.' His eyes gleamed down at her. 'Satisfied now, Miss Marnie Hamilton?'

She wasn't, but there was no alternative than to pretend to be. 'I suppose,' she answered half-heartedly.

Conrad muttered something under his breath and she gave him a disdainful glance. Something resembling a smile crossed his lips and Marnie found herself relaxing—a bit.

Conrad parked the ute. 'I'll get the gardener to help set up the tree. I know you're bursting to check on Eva so off you go.'

'Yoo-hoo-o-o.' Eva's voice.

Marnie and Conrad swung around. Eva was rocking in her chair looking as fresh and as bright as a daisy. Annie was walking from the patio with a tray in her hands. She had been delivering tall glasses of freshly made lime juice. Sitting beside Eva with Eva's favourite book of poetry was Helena.

Conrad glanced triumphantly down at Marnie's startled features. It was obvious Helena had been reading to Eva. And it was equally obvious that Eva had enjoyed every minute of it!

CHAPTER SEVEN

HELENA came towards them, followed by Eva. Eva was walking with the aid of a walking stick, something which Marnie had never seen her use before. Her beautiful hair-do had been brushed severely back, spoiling all the curl, and was held in place by several hair pins. Her frail frame was draped in a dress that must have looked beautiful on her when she was many years younger and several pounds heavier. Now the beige frock only robbed her of the little colour she had left and made her look much older than her eighty-odd years. Older and weaker. The walking stick and flattened hair-do made her seem like a candidate for a nursing home where the inmates supped their meals through straws and slept in cots with the sides rolled up.

Helena in comparison was a vision of loveliness as she swept towards them, her long blonde hair flowing across her shoulders and the emerald green sundress with its splashes of red and white colouring making her seem packed with energy and youthful vitality. Eva's book of poetry was still in her hands as she came up to Conrad. ' "How do I love thee, let me ⸺ ⸺ the ways",' she laughingly quoted as she wrappe⸺ ⸺ ⸺ound his neck and waited for his kiss w⸺ coming.

Conrad planted a sound kiss o⸺ and then, chuckling, removed he⸺ neck. Marnie had turned awa⸺ brazen show of affection. Tea⸺ watched Eva walk stiffly tow⸺

11

did indeed need the walking stick. The power of suggestion Marnie thought grimly as she quickly made her way towards the older woman.

Brushing her tears aside so Eva wouldn't notice, Marnie put an arm around the bony shoulders and smiled down into the lined face. Eva loved a bit of make-up but Marnie saw now that not a trace of lispstick or powder could be seen.

'Have you had breakfast?' Marnie softly asked her, only to be overheard by Helena.

'Of course she's had breakfast,' Helena snapped, her green eyes frosty as she looked at Marnie. 'Even though Conrad is paying *you* good money to look after her it was *me* who had to perform the honours this morning.'

'Easy, Helena,' Conrad put in. 'It wasn't Marnie's fault that she wasn't here this morning. I thought it would simplify matters if we ducked off to get the tree and the meats. But thank you for looking after Grandmother,' he said, his eyes smiling across at Eva.

Marnie held her breath waiting for Helena to protest that she hadn't been included in the excursion, but when none was forthcoming and as Helena wasn't paying any attention to the tree Conrad was showing to his grandmother, Marnie decided that tree buying wasn't high on Helena's priority list of exciting happenings.

'Cooking an egg isn't any big deal,' Helena continued in a waspish manner. 'Flora would have done it but she and Annie have been busy all morning dusting and vacuuming. Really, Conrad, I think you should have hired some domestics for over the holidays. I don't see how Flora is going to cope with all the guests and are meals besides. I can tell you they're not very bout the whole situation and we were discussing perhaps Marnie here should pitch in and

'Marnie has her job,' Conrad told her flatly, 'and Flora and Annie know what their jobs are. Besides, we will all be helping in our own ways. I'm doing the barbecue and you said you would look after the salads. That leaves Flora and Annie free for any jobs that need catching up.'

'I haven't had a chance to even think about salads,' Helena stormed angrily. 'How was I to know that you would go sneaking off with ... with *her* this morning and leave me your grandmother to look after. She can't do a thing for herself. I had to dress her and do her hair and break her egg into tiny bits and practically feed her. And if that wasn't enough I had to read to her!'

Marnie saw Conrad stiffen with anger and his black eyes shone with barely concealed rage. Helena saw it too and knowing she had gone too far, burst into tears. She flung herself against Conrad, sobbing against his chest. Conrad's arms hung stiffly by his sides as he made no attempt to placate her.

Putting her arm around Eva, Marnie led her quietly into the house and upstairs to her bedroom. Once upstairs and in the safety of her room Eva began to cry. Not like Helena had cried, with loud sobbing bursts, but quietly, hopelessly, as if her heart had broken and no one seemed to care. Marnie held her in her arms and rocked her gently back and forth, soothing her and comforting her with softly spoken words.

Marnie looked up to find Conrad standing at the door. She had no idea how long he had been standing there but she saw the pain in his eyes as he watched his grandmother. Marnie got up and left the room knowing this would be a good time for them to be left alone. Eva needed the reassurance that only her grandson could give her.

She went to her room and telephoned her aunt,

apologising for not being able to make it for Christmas dinner and telling her that everything was fine and she would see her as soon as possible. After wishing everyone all the best for a happy Christmas Marnie hung up the telephone and sat on her bed, staring across the room. She wondered what Conrad and his grandmother were talking about while visions of Eva walking with her cane came back to her, starting up a fresh wave of anger. She should never have left Eva alone and she blamed herself for Eva's present misery.

There was a light rapping on her door. Before she had a chance to cross the room to answer it the door opened and Conrad came in. He stood by the door, a closed expression on his face. What was he thinking, Marnie found herself wondering as he remained standing by the door.

'How is Eva?' she asked softly, wanting to go over to him but remaining standing where she was.

He ran a hand through his hair and shut the door behind him before answering. 'She's resting. I think she'll sleep for a couple of hours What did you say to her to make her cry? I've never seen her so upset!'

Marnie's eyes widened in disbelief. 'What did *I* say to her?' she gasped.

He walked over and stood in front of the window. Marnie could hear voices and laughter floating through the opened french doors. The guests had arrived! 'Damn!' he muttered savagely. 'Where did all those people come from?'

Marnie walked over to stand beside him. There were several people gathered around the pool She counted quickly. Fourteen men and women of various shapes and sizes and more arriving. Helena was ushering them into the patio surrounding the pool, kissing and hugging each guest as they arrived.

Conrad stood with his hands in his pockets glowering down at them.

'You're not forgetting they are your guests?' Marnie asked him. 'The guests you and Helena have been constantly referring to? The guests you wanted to rush back for so you could shave and prepare the barbecue? The guests you didn't want Helena to have to welcome on her own? The guests you hired me for to keep your grandmother out of their way?'

'I've never laid eyes on any of those people before,' he growled impatiently. 'Damn that Helena anyway. I warned her not to go over my head and invite those blasted friends of hers.'

Marnie turned away from the window and crossed the room. 'It seems,' she said, opening the door and standing beside it, 'that Helena does pretty much as she pleases around here and no one dares object!'

He turned from the window and looked at her, quiet censure in his eyes. She met his gaze unflinchingly, the opened door telling him better than any words that she wanted him to leave.

His long legs ate up the distance separating them. He put his hand on the door and looked down at her. 'You had better go,' she said quickly before he had a chance to speak. 'Helena will be wondering where you are.'

A muscle jerked spasmodically alongside his jaw and his lips tightened into a thin, forbidding line. Without a word he stepped into the hall.

'And just for the record,' Marnie managed to throw in before he had a chance to walk away, 'I didn't say anything to upset Eva. When you came into her bedroom I was comforting her not upsetting her.' She shut the door quickly and leaned against it. Her breathing was coming in rapid gasps. She waited several minutes before she felt calm enough to walk back to the window. She shook her head in disbelief. There were now more than forty people gathered around the pool. No wonder Helena thought Conrad should have hired some domestics! Marnie watched her, quietly shaking her head. The way Helena was behaving anyone would think the house, the pool, the whole estate belonged to her. Marnie moved from the window, her eyes reflecting her misery. Probably some day it would, she dared to admit, and when that day happened there would never by any peace for Eva or any happiness. Her heart dropped to the pit of her stomach because she knew there wouldn't be any peace or happiness for Conrad either.

How could he be so blind? she thought sadly. How could he be fooled by Helena's treacherous ways, her meaness and her nastiness? It just seemed incredible that he would put up with her. She flopped across her bed and rested her cheek against her arm while tears trickled slowly on to the bedspread. He puts up with her because he loves her and if you loved someone enough then you would always find excuses to explain away their behaviour. Her eyelids grew heavy and she closed them, hoping for sleep and blessed relief from her torturous thoughts.

When she awoke it was to the tantalising aroma of steaks sizzling on a barbecue. She got up and padded across to the french doors. Her eyes fell on Conrad immediately. Despite the obvious reluctance he had displayed earlier over the unwanted number of guests, he was being the perfect host. He was dressed in white shorts and T-shirt which showed off his lean masculinity and deep tan. It was easy to see he was relaxed and several times his deep throated laughter carried up to her room. She supposed she should be glad he was relaxing after having worked so hard with such long hours but perversely every time his laughter sounded she found her hands clenching into tight fists.

And just as perversely she found she couldn't tear herself away from the french windows. Her eyes followed him around the patio, straining to see who it was he was speaking with or who it was he was sharing a joke with. Not that it mattered who he spoke with or laughed with, she tried to tell herself, because after all she didn't know any of these people, who or what they were or where they came from.

Helena, she noticed, followed him around as if she was terrified of losing sight of him for even one minute, and Marnie could see why. It was obvious Conrad was the object of more than one girl's pretty sights and, rogue that he was, he was perfectly aware of the attention he was receiving. Judging by the manner in which he casually handled it, he was quite accustomed to having women literally flinging themselves at him.

Marnie finally turned away in disgust. While he was downstairs having the time of his life she and Eva were trapped upstairs with nothing to do. She let herself out of her room to peek in on Eva. The darling was still asleep. Marnie went back to her own room and took a shower, giving her hair a shampoo at the same time. After dressing in a bright lemon-yellow sun suit and applying just a delicate touch of make-up she again went to check on Eva. This time she was awake.

To Marnie's amazement Eva was in good spirits and had apparently forgotten her earlier upset, her primary concern being what had happened to her hair-do.

'A set should last longer than this!' she wailed in despair, looking at herself in the mirror.

'Have your bath,' Marnie told her, 'and then we'll see what we can do with it.'

But try as they might Eva's fine hair couldn't be restored to its earlier beauty.

'I'll just have to have it done again,' Eva said firmly. 'I can't go through Christmas looking like *this*!'

'Well, we might try Palm Beach,' Marnie suggested. 'There should be a salon there.'

'There is,' Eva declared emphatically. 'It's just a small place but I used to go there all the time . . . years ago.'

But would it still be there Marnie wondered as she helped Eva into a becoming summer frock of pale blue cotton. As she did up the zipper of Eva's dress music from downstairs drifted through to them.

'What is that racket?' Eva demanded to know, her eyes puzzled as she turned to Marnie.

'There's a party going on downstairs,' Marnie told her. 'A pool party and barbecue.'

'Oh,' Eva sighed. 'The Christmas celebrations have started then, and me with my hair looking like this. I hope we don't run into anyone before I get it set again.'

'I'm sure we won't,' Marnie smiled. 'Everyone is occupied around the pool'

Conrad met them at the foot of the stairs. 'I was just coming up to get you,' he said, his black eyes running over Marnie's pert little figure. 'Get into your bikini and come and join us.' He turned to his grandmother. 'I've set up a special lounge chair for you,' he said with a wink. 'Under the biggest umbrella, where you can have a bird's eye view of the whole proccedings.'

Eva's eyes widened with pleasure. 'How nice of you, dear,' she enthused, clasping her hands in front of her like a young girl. 'But . . . but are you quite certain I won't be in the way?'

'Quite certain,' he assured her warmly, taking her thin little arm in his hand. He turned to Marnie and tucked her arm into his as well. 'Shall we join the party, ladies?' he asked in a grand manner.

'Oh dear,' Eva sighed, putting her free hand to her hair. 'We can't just now. You see Marnie and I were just going to take a wee drive to Palm Beach. It's my hair you know. Something has happened to it and I must have it set again.'

Conrad studied her hair. 'Your hair looks just fine to me,' he said. 'In fact you look lovely. I like that dress you're wearing.'

Eva's eyes shone with pleasure and gratitude while a faint smudge of colour stained her cheeks. 'Marnie picked this dress out for me. You bought it for me last year Conrad when you were in London.' Her eyes twinkled mischieviously. 'I do believe you have forgotten.'

He studied the dress and slowly shook his head. 'Sometimes your memory astounds me, Grandmother,' he said with a chuckle. 'Yes, that is the dress I bought for you when I was in London, but it's the first time I've ever seen you wearing it.'

'It's the first time I've worn it,' Eva admitted apologetically, 'but I'm glad now because it's still like new and it fits so much better than my old frocks.'

Marnie dared a glance at Conrad and she saw the blood rush to his face while guilt flashed briefly in his eyes. 'I'm sorry, Grandmother,' he said softly, 'I should have seen to it that your wardrobe was kept up to date.'

'Don't be silly,' Eva rebuked him. 'What do men know about such things?' But Marnie could see that Eva was pleased with her grandson's concern. Her eyes met Conrad's across the snow white hair and they smiled. Their smiles were tinged with sadness because they knew Eva had been neglected and that she shouldn't have been.

'Well, from now on young lady,' he scolded his grandmother, 'we go shopping at least once a year.' Marnie caught his eye again and he grinned sheepishly. 'Well, maybe more often than that. Maybe twice a year.'

'And when will you find time for that?' his grandmother scolded him in return. 'What with your office down town and your study here, not to mention the telephone and your construction sites, I can't see you finding time to take an old lady shopping. Of course, if I had *another* grandson and if that grandson were smarter than you then he would find a nice girl like Marnie here and marry her and *she* would take me shopping.'

Marnie's cheeks flamed with burning colour. 'Eva!' she blurted without thinking, aware of Conrad's eyes boring into her. She dared to glance up at him and she was startled by the look in his eyes.

'Judging from Marnie's reaction to your suggestion, Grandmother, I would say it's indeed fortunate that you don't have another grandson,' he said quietly.

He didn't add that Marnie was far too critical of the Wright's to want to join them but Marnie knew that was what he was thinking. It was all there in his eyes and she read his message loud and clear. She swallowed the lump in her throat and forced a bright smile on her face.

'Well, if we're going to have your hair set, Eva, we had better be getting a move on.'

Marnie thought Conrad would object. Instead he released both their arms and said grimly. 'Yes, you might as well take advantage of Marnie's services while you can. She's only here until the end of summer you know.' His eyes were cruelly mocking as he raked Marnie's face which had gone suddenly pale. For Eva's sake she bit back the sharp retort which hovered on her lips and said instead.

'Yes, that's right, but the end of summer is a long way off and so both of you will have the pleasure of my company for quite a while yet.' She tried to give Conrad a scathing glance but failed dismally. She only managed to look wistful and lonely. Conrad's eyes hardened on that look but she dragged her eyes away before he could read anything into it. It wouldn't do to have him think that it wasn't only Eva who could take advantage of her services!

'*Conrad!*' Helena rushed towards them, her calculating green eyes going from face to face. 'Conrad!' she repeated his name once more, her long, red-tipped fingers clutching at his arm. 'Have you forgotten our guests? Everyone is wondering where you are. You must come immediately before the party dies out.'

'I'll be right with you,' he said, unobtrusively removing his arm from Helena's clutches. 'I came in to try and get Grandmother and Marnie to join us.'

Helena stared at him as if he had suddenly lost all leave of his senses. 'You *what*?' she gasped.

'Don't worry,' he coldly informed her, 'they have better things to do. It seems another hair-do is in order. Or at least,' he turned to go, 'that's the excuse offered.'

Marnie watched him go, broad shoulders held straight and the proud arrogant head held high. When she turned, it was to find Helena's eyes on her.

'I see you're still trying to get him to notice you,' she offered cruelly, a smug look in her eyes. 'I thought at first you were using his grandmother as an excuse to get to him but I can see now I was wrong.' Her eyes turned to Eva and then swung back to Marnie. 'The old girl is proving useful after all. With that dreadful hair of hers and with your willingness to oblige, the two of you seem to spend most of your time at the beauty parlour!' Her eyes skimmed over Marnie's short cut. 'How you can stand that style of yours, I shall never know.' Then with a toss of her own luxuriously long hair Helena turned on her heel and hurried to catch up to Conrad.

'Never mind her,' Eva said kindly. 'I think your hair is very nice. It looks clean and fresh,' she added, as though this in itself was the extreme compliment.

Marnie smiled. 'Thanks, Eva,' she said. 'Do you want something to eat before we go or should we grab something at Palm Beach?'

'Let's get something at Palm Beach,' Eva said and with this decided, off they went.

The beauty parlour Eva remembered was no longer operating, but as it turned out there were several others to choose from, only this time they had to wait before they could get an appointment. So they whiled away the time by having soup and sandwiches at a pavement café and watching the tourists as they strolled by with camera bags and binoculars swinging around their necks or over their shoulders. Christmas carols filled the air and every available tree was decorated gaily. It was pleasant, picturesque and happy, but Marnie was feeling anything but happy.

Her thoughts were with Conrad as she sadly stirred her ice cream soda. It seemed that everything she said or did was misconstrued by him. Eva's hand covered hers and she started guiltily.

'Oh, I'm sorry, Eva.' She glanced quickly at her watch. 'I must have been daydreaming. Is it time to go?'

'No, we still have some time left before my appointment,' Eva assured her, 'but I was wondering about you. What's wrong, child?' she asked softly. 'What makes you so, well, unhappy?'

Tears sprang to Marnie's eyes and she quickly brushed them away. 'It's ... it's the time of year, I guess. The carols and ... and the trees all decorated.'

'And that's what makes you unhappy?' Eva asked shrewdly. 'You're sure it isn't what Helena said? You mustn't let her bother you, Marnie. Take a lesson from me.'

'No, it's not Helena, although she is trying at times,' she sighed, thinking she had just made the understatement of the year. She bent her head and sipped at her soda. 'Conrad doesn't seem very happy with his guests,' she remarked.

'He doesn't like Helena's friends,' Eva told her. 'She's a model you know and her friends are all the artsy types. He'll be happier when his own friends arrive. They should be there by the time we get back.'

Marnie's eyes widened in surprise. 'His and hers guests?'

Eva chuckled. 'You might say that,' she agreed. 'They say opposites attract, but if you want my opinion Helena is not the right young woman for my grandson. And you know what else I think?' She leaned closer to Marnie and whispered. 'I don't think Helena loves him. I think she's after his money!'

Marnie pretended to be shocked. *'No!'*

'*Yes!* And you know what else I think? I think he doesn't love Helena! I think he just hasn't bothered to take the time to get rid of her.'

Marnie's heart flooded with happiness. Could it be true? she wondered hopefully. She had long guessed that Helena couldn't love anyone other than herself and several times she had noticed that Conrad certainly didn't behave like a man should who is in love. But at the same time she couldn't really believe he would put up with someone for as long as he had put up with Helena if he didn't love her. Her sudden burst of happiness began to dwindle. The light from her eyes faded. Helena might not be the girl for Conrad but then neither was she. They lived in two different worlds and never saw eye to eye on anything. Suddenly the end of summer seemed a long time away and she knew it was going to be unbearably painful to be so close to Conrad and yet so far away.

It was dark before Marnie and Eva finally got home. After Eva's appointment with the hairdressers they had driven into Sydney to Marnies' aunt's place and had allowed themselves to be talked into having dinner with the family. Eva was the centre of attention, amusing them with stories of past Christmases, and it was all Marnie could do to drag her away from her attentive audience. Marnie had rung and spoken to Flora, telling her that they were staying in town and wouldn't be home until around nine.

The music was louder now and Marnie and Eva could hear it before they saw the house. As they made the turn in the driveway the huge home appeared before them, lit up like a Christmas tree. Every light in the house was blazing, both upstairs and down. Outdoor lights flooded the gardens and the lawns and shouts of laughter and splashing could be heard coming from the pool area.

Cars crammed the circular driveway near the garage and it was all Marnie could do to find a small section where she could squeeze her car in. Eva was tired, and sagged against Marnie as they made their way towards the opened front door. The music was almost deafening as they stepped into the entrance hall. Conrad appeared as if by magic from the sun room and Marnie was startled by his appearance and by the fact he wasn't with his friends celebrating by the pool side. She looked beyond him, expecting to see Helena with him; that perhaps they had gone to the sun room to be alone for a few minutes.

But Helena was nowhere to be seen and Conrad had the attitude of a man who had been alone for quite some time. He had changed out of his shorts and was now wearing a pair of casual summer slacks, fawn coloured and topped with a lightweight V-necked jumper of a creamy colour. Marnie's heart leapt at the sight of him but she carefully masked her feelings, her expression calm as she looked at him.

His face was in shadows so Marnie sensed rather

than saw that he was angry. She stiffened and her arm tightened around Eva's shoulders.

'What's the idea of keeping my grandmother out until this hour?' he demanded in an ominous tone. 'Where the hell have you been?'

'Conrad!' his grandmother gasped. 'That's no way to speak to Marnie. We've had a wonderful time.'

'And causing everyone to worry about you in the process,' he snapped, his voice bristling in anger. But he wasn't talking to his grandmother. His eyes were riveted on Marnie's face. 'I've been up and down the road looking for you. I thought you might have had an accident or a flat tyre or something. You've been gone for hours.'

'I'm sorry if we . . .' Marnie began, but he didn't give her the opportunity to finish. He stepped out of the shadows and she almost recoiled against the fury she saw in his eyes and in his distorted features.

'Sorry?' he snarled menacingly. 'Sorry?' he repeated again, this time his voice sounding flat. Marnie moistened her lips and stared helplessly up at him. 'Sorry that I've been half out of mind worrying about you? Do you realise I was just about to ring the police? Ten more minutes and I would have.'

'But didn't Flora give you my message?' Marnie asked desperately. 'I rang and told her to tell you that we would be staying in Sydney for dinner.'

His eyes narrowed. 'Dinner? Until this hour? Who were you with?'

Marnie was becoming resentful. She would dearly have loved to say that she and Eva had been escorted by two divinely charming men to one of Sydney's most exclusive restaurants, but in Conrad's present mood she knew that would be unwise.

'We were at my aunt's and uncle's. They invited us for dinner and we accepted. I rang and told Flora.'

Marnie hesitated and then added. 'I really am sorry that you didn't receive the message. Eva and I didn't mean to worry you.'

Conrad's shoulders slumped as he shoved his hands into his pockets and she could tell that his anger was slowly leaving his body, making him appear heart-breakingly vulnerable. It was only after he had pulled one of his hands from his pocket to drag it slowly through the thick, almost untidy scrub of his jet black hair, did she understand the terrible strain he had been through.

And even though Flora hadn't relayed her message as she should have, Marnie held herself responsible for the worry she had caused him. She should have insisted on speaking to Conrad himself and not trusted Flora to do anything on hers and Eva's behalf. She should have realised Flora wasn't to be trusted, not even for the simple task of passing on a telephone message.

But if she thought Conrad would accept her apology she was sadly mistaken. His anger might have left him but that was all. He was still clearly annoyed that she had caused him so much trouble.

'I don't want you on the roads during the holiday season,' he informed her curtly. 'The roads are crowded with drunks this time of year. If you must go somewhere then I will drive you.'

Marnie gaped at him. Did he really believe that he could practically keep her prisoner here? Because that's exactly how she saw it, for she knew she would never ask him to drive her around whenever she and Eva felt the need to get away for awhile.

'That won't be necessary,' Marnie protested. 'I've been driving for years and have never had an accident. Not even a dent or a bump.'

'There's always a first time,' he remarked drily, 'and since it is my grandmother's welfare at stake, then I must insist that you stay off the roads, at least until after New Year.'

Marnie raised her hands and then dropped them. 'But you're being unreasonable,' she flared, her nerve ends stretched to the limit. 'I tell you I'm a very careful driver. Each year I enrol in a Defensive Driving course. I am probably,' she dared to say it, 'a better driver than you! At least,' she continued bravely, 'I would never dream of *speeding*!'

A deep flush spread across his cheek bones as he remembered how Marnie had begged him to slow down on their way back from Manly with the tree and the turkey. Her violet coloured eyes sparkled with triumph and a faint smile dimpled the corners of her mouth.

Eva tugged at her arm. 'Conrad's right, Marnie,' she said. 'The roads are dangerous this time of year. It's best not to be on them unless it's an emergency.'

'It would seem,' Conrad drawled to his grandmother, 'that Marnie could take some lessons from you in common sense.' His eyes slanted down at Marnie's upturned face. 'She apparently has had one lesson too many on how to be defensive!' He held up one large hand to silence her as her lips parted in protest. 'Don't argue with me, Marnie, just do as I say. I don't want you on the roads and that's final. I've got better things to do than occupy my time worrying whether you've been involved in a smash-up.'

His tone and manner of speaking indicated that the discussion was over, but Marnie wasn't about to give up her freedom so easily. Nor was she about to allow this overbearing, arrogant brute of a man to dictate to her. She was an excellent driver and didn't believe in taking unnecessary risks with her life or that of any other person on the road. Being a school teacher, the only time she had the freedom to really drive was on school vacations .... like now. And no one was going to take that liberty away from her.

'Short of taking my keys away from me,' she stubbornly pursued the subject, 'then I can't see how you can possibly keep me from driving my car when and where I please.'

His eyes ignited into flames. 'Are your keys in your car now?' he asked her, the soft tones of his voice making him sound somehow sinister.

Marnie hesitated, unsure of what her answer should be.

'Well, are they?' he demanded again in that soft voice which scraped along her nerves.

Marnie raised her chin in defiance. 'I never leave my keys in the ignition,' she told him.

'Then they must be in your handbag,' he suggested casually.

'Of course!'

'Give them to me.'

'What!'

He held out his hand. 'Give me your car keys.' There was no mistaking the warning note which ran through his voice. Marnie shook her head and backed away from him, clutching her handbag firmly against her chest. 'Don't be ridiculous,' she snapped. 'You have no business demanding my keys.'

'I have every right to demand possession of them,' he informed her coldly. 'While you are in my employ I am responsible for you. Now give me those keys or so help me I'll take them from you.'

Marnie darted a quick look at Eva and to her amazement Eva appeared to be enjoying this confrontation between Marnie and her grandson. Marnie licked her lips in bewilderment. It was partly for her own independence that she refused to have Conrad take away her driving privileges but mostly it was because Marnie honestly believed Eva needed the stimulation of being taken out and enjoying the company of others.

Without a car, all that would come to an end. Therefore, Marnie was rather surprised that Eva wasn't openly on her side. Not that Marnie wanted to drag Eva into an argument against Conrad, but she felt Eva should have offered a faint protest or two against her grandson's unreasonable behaviour.

Marnie glared up at him, still holding her handbag protectively against her chest. 'I ... I promise I won't take the car out unless I first tell you,' she offered in a tight voice.

He snapped his fingers. 'The keys, Marnie. NOW!'

'Oh, all right,' she flushed angrily, fumbling through her bag while tears of outrage pricked behind her eyelids.

He snatched the bag from her trembling hands and reached inside, coming out with her keys dangling from his fingers. He tossed them into the air, caught them and then pocketed them while Marnie watched in undisguised contempt.

He handed her back her handbag and as she reached for it their hands touched. Marnie jerked her hand away as though he had somehow managed to burn it.

'Good night, Marnie ... Eva.' He turned and walked away from them, but not before Marnie had caught the triumphant gleam shining from his eyes.

CHAPTER EIGHT

IT was Christmas Eve. The house was very quiet as Marnie strolled through it, marvelling at how beautiful everything appeared. She had offered her services to Flora and Annie and Flora had only hesitated briefly before accepting an extra pair of hands. And so Marnie had spent most of that day dusting and polishing and vacuuming while Conrad and his guests relaxed around the pool or went swimming in the surf.

The tree had been put in the main lounge room and as far as Marnie knew no attempts had been made to decorate it. She felt oddly disappointed that Conrad's enthusiam for the tree had been so short-lived. She made her way now to the lounge, wishing she had had her car so she could have nipped into Paddington to get her own Christmas decorations and decorate the tree herself. She had asked Eva where their decorations were but Eva hadn't known, saying they had probably been thrown out or given away.

The door to the lounge was closed and Marnie opened it not expecting to find anyone there. But someone was! Conrad was sitting in the middle of the floor surrounded by Christmas tree lights. So absorbed was he in testing the tiny globes that he didn't hear or notice Marnie standing just inside the door. His dark head was bent forward, his hair falling over his forehead. Beside him was a huge box and from the box he had removed a dazzling assortment of decorations. There was a peaceful expression on his face and he looked for all the world like a small boy who had been reunited with his toy box.

Marnie watched him, a tender smile curving the soft lines of her mouth. He looked up suddenly and the almost boyish expression disappeared from his face, the hard, ruthless lines appearing like magic across his features and her heart sank at the all too familiar guarded look.

'Hi,' she greeted him, closing the door behind her and leaning against it.

He nodded a greeting and returned to his work. Marnie didn't wait to be invited to help him. Men like Conrad Wright didn't ask for or expect to receive help. She crossed the room and sat down beside him, watching as his huge hands gently grasped the tiny globes and inserted them into a testing bank.

'I've never seen such beautiful decorations,' she said at last. 'Do you mind if I examine some of them?'

'Help yourself. Just be careful though. They're old and therefore fragile.'

Marnie's cheeks flushed at his tone. Did he think she was a bull in a china shop? Nevertheless she was extremely careful as she handled the glass baubles for they were indeed extremely fragile just as he had warned. She looked up at the tree and she fervently wished it could have been nicer. He caught the expression on her face and smiled.

'I know what you're thinking, but wait until it's decorated. Here,' he said, handing her some gold-coloured tinsel, 'see what you can do with this while I string the lights on.'

The tinsel was the real thing, long strips of metal, but terribly tangled. By the time Marnie had managed to unravel them, Conrad had strung the tree with the lights.

'How does that look?' he asked, his voice ringing with enthusiasm which caused a ready grin to spring to Marnie's lips.

'Like a Christmas tree *should*!' she announced

promptly, her eyes glowing as brightly as the globes on the tree. His own eyes sparkled down at her as she gazed excitedly up at the tree.

He took the tinsel from her hands and spread it carefully over the back of a chair. 'We'll get the ornaments on now,' he said, 'and then we'll put on the tinsel.'

They worked in companionable silence, listening to the carols which were playing on the stereo, sometimes humming along to the old familiar favourites. When the tree was completely decorated they stood back and admired their masterpiece. For it was a masterpiece, so carefully and so lovingly had it been decorated with the beautiful antique figurines.

'Oh, dear!' Marnie exclaimed. 'We need something for the top!'

'Ah, ha!' His eyes were filled with a devilish delight as he smiled down into her face. 'I was wondering when you would notice that!' He crossed over to the huge box and picked up the final ornament. It was carefully wrapped in brown paper and tied together with a neat bow. Marnie watched curiously as he painstakingly unwrapped it, almost as if the wrapping and the cord it was tied with was as precious as the contents it protected.

At last he stood in front of her, the ornament in his hands. It was a star. It was three dimensional and Marnie knew without having been told that it was made of the finest, softest gold. She shook her head in wonder and lifted her violet eyes to his. The star was reflected in his eyes as he gazed down at her and there was a hint of sadness in their black depths.

'My great-grandfather brought this with him when he left England to make a new life for himself and his bride in Australia,' he said softly. 'It was to be a symbol of their love for each other and of their hope for the future.' His voice took on a raw, almost painful edge and it was filled with emotion. 'I never truly understood what it was supposed to symbolise . . . until now!'

Marnie's heart was pounding so fiercely she thought he must surely hear it. He held the star out to her and she touched it, her fingers trembling.

'It . . . It's beautiful,' she murmured huskily, her eyes on his.

'And what it stands for?' he queried softly, his eyes holding hers.

'Yes, yes,' she agreed, 'especially for what it stands for!'

'Marnie?' There was a question in his voice, a kind of desperation as he said her name.

'Y-Yes?' She looked appealingly up at him, her heart fluttering in her throat as his mouth moved tantalisingly close to hers.

'Marnie, I . . .'

But he was never able to finish what he had been trying to say. A door slammed in the hallway and the sharp click of a woman's high heels could be heard rushing towards the lounge. The door was flung open and Helena stood there, her green eyes blazing with anger. She looked slightly dishevelled and it was easy to see she had been drinking. The tree was blazing with all it's lights, but she paid it not the slightest attention. She slammed the door behind her and marched across the room to stand in front of Conrad. Whisky fumes and the stale odour of cigarettes formed a vapour around her and Marnie moved away to begin picking up discarded paper and tinsel to put in the box.

'How dare you keep me waiting like this,' Helena screeched at Conrad. 'You said you would only be an hour and it's been more like *three*!'

'Easy, Helena,' Conrad returned in a tired voice.

'Easy, Helena! Easy, Helena!' she mimicked him, her voice harsh and grating. 'Is that all you can say?' She whirled towards Marnie. 'I bet it's your fault he's still here instead of at the beach party with *me*!' She flung herself back at Conrad. 'Don't you realise everyone is *talking*? They're wondering why you spend so much of your time with *her* instead of with *me*! Well, I won't stand for it, Conrad, I . . .'

Marnie had turned away from this humiliating scene but her head snapped around at the sounds of a scuffle and she watched in horrified dismay as Conrad picked Helena up and tossed her kicking and screaming across his shoulder and calmly walked with her out of the room.

Completely shaken, Marnie stood rooted to the spot staring at the door long after it had been closed and Helena's screeches had died away. It was after she had regained her composure that she noticed the star lying on the floor. She knelt beside it and her hands slowly reached for it, picking it up to press against her chest. What had he been about to say she wondered, before they had been so rudely interrupted? Had he been about to tell her that he *loved* her? Her heart somersaulted in her chest and she squeezed her eyes shut. 'Oh, Conrad,' she whispered, 'I love you so. Could it be that you . . . that you love me? Dare I hope that that's what you wanted to say?'

She opened her eyes and looked up at the tree, the star still in her hands and still folded to her breast. Conrad had said it was a symbol of hope . . . of love. Did he hope that she loved him? Was he allowing the star to speak for himself? Could it be possible that a man like Conrad Wright found it hard, maybe impossible to express his love in mere words? She thought of his grandmother and knew without doubt that he loved her, but she was almost certain that he hadn't actually told her, at least not in so many words.

Footsteps sounded in the hall and she knew it was

Conrad returning. Her heart almost stopped beating and then beat so rapidly she felt almost breathless. She got slowly to her feet, still clutching the star. Her face was pale as she faced the door. Somehow it was very important that she correctly read the expression on his face. *Is he friend, or is he foe?* a childhood rhyme came back to her, whirling like a tornado in her brain.

The door opened and her heart sank. He was foe! The all-too familiar hard lines of his face telling her he was fed up with women! Her heart filled with despair and tears threatened to blind her as she turned away from him towards the tree.

'Is . . . is Helena all right, now?' she asked in a small voice, pretending great interest in the tree. The lights blurred in front of her but she dared not wipe her tears away because she realised he hadn't seen them and any tell-tale action would only give her away. He had probably had to contend with Helena's tears and had had his fill of those as well.

'Yes,' he answered brusquely behind her, 'she will be all right in the morning. Too much grog, I'm afraid. It wasn't her fault. I lost all track of time. I should have been down at the party to . . . to keep an eye on her.'

He sounded miserable and she wondered if he was half as miserable as she felt. 'Are . . . are you going now? To the party I mean?'

'No, it will be wrapping up soon. Everyone has had a big day.' He came up beside her. She could see the black jumper he had on, his sleeves rolled up and the strong muscular forearms folded across his chest as he looked up at the tree. Marnie handed him the star without actually looking at him. He accepted it without actually looking at her. They were both holding their breaths but neither knew about the other. The only thing they did know was that their magic moment had passed. Helena had effectively robbed them of that.

They had used a small step ladder to reach the highest branches and now Conrad dragged it forward and stood on the bottom rung as he stretched and placed the star on top of the tree. He stood very still, his head raised to the star and Marnie knew he was thinking of his great-grandfather who had carried this star from one country to shine in this, the other country.

Marnie helped him tidy up the room. It only took a few minutes but it seemed to take forever, both of them lost in their own private thoughts. There was no humming. When they had finished, Marnie said in an extremely calm voice as though nothing had happened between them, nothing at all.

'Your grandmother is upstairs resting. She would like to go to church tonight. To the midnight Carol Service.'

They stared at each other like strangers. 'I'll take her.'

'You're tired,' Marnie protested. 'I'll take her.'

'How? I've got your keys and I don't intend giving them back. There will be drunks around. It's not safe.'

They were still staring at each other. Their looks were impersonal, but both were reluctant to look away. They were caught in a whirlpool, and were helpless against it.

'I hadn't planned to ask you for my keys,' she told him steadily, hearing her voice playing like a recording in her ears. 'We had planned to take a taxi.'

He sucked in his breath. 'If I hadn't been here tonight, if I had gone to the party you would have left without telling me?'

She raised her hands as if in some sort of protest but they felt heavy and she dropped them, letting them hang like dead weights at her sides.

'Yes,' she answered honestly. 'Yes, we would have gone without your knowing.' She cleared her throat. 'I haven't seen you all day. You ... were with your friends.' *With Helena*!

'You could have joined us. I wanted you to.'

'Yes . . . yes, I know that but . . . but . . .' Her voice trailed off. How could she tell him that it was nothing short of agony to see him with Helena?

'Never mind,' he cut in sharply, a hooded expression in his eyes. 'I told you that if you wanted to go anywhere, I would be only too happy to drive you.'

'Yes, I know, but I didn't want to disturb you.' How could she have gone up to him in the middle of his guests and asked if he would be available that evening to take them to church? And if Helena had been nearby, which she most surely would have been, then she would have wanted to know why she couldn't drive to church herself. It would have been humiliating to have to reveal that Conrad had confiscated her car keys.

'I would have been more disturbed to come home and find you missing. Hadn't you considered that?'

Marnie bowed her head, the light shining on the smooth cap of her hair causing it to shimmer with red highlights. She traced a pattern on the rug with the toe of her shoe. 'I didn't think you would notice . . . or care,' she finally admitted in a low voice.

He cupped her chin with his hand and forced her to meet his eyes. 'I'm not as callous and as uncaring as you apparently think I am,' he said gruffly. 'I . . . would have known you weren't in the house.'

Her eyes widened. 'But how?' she asked breathlessly.

His eyes hardened. 'I would have known!' His hand moved up to her cheek, his fingers lightly caressing the smooth surface. 'If we're going to church you had better get grandmother ready. It will soon be midnight.' He took his hand away and stood back from her, his eyes still on the delicate beauty of her perfect features. 'I'll wait for you in the entrance hall.'

Eva was ready when Marnie got up to her room. She had assembled all her Christmas gifts and had them piled on her bed. Around her shoulders was a beautiful mink stole and perched on her new hair-do was a small mink beret. Eva was the picture of elegance and Marnie wasted no time in telling her so. Eva was pleased and as Marnie looked at her she found it hard to remember what Eva had looked like when she first came to be her companion. Eva had regained most of her self-confidence, and it showed by making her appear years younger than she actually was.

'I'm glad you've got your gifts ready, Eva,' Marnie said with a twinkle in her eyes. 'I'll go and fetch mine and we'll take them downstairs. There's a surprise waiting for you.'

'Don't tell me the tree has been decorated?' Eva asked in a disbelieving voice. 'I saw it today and nothing had been done. Where did you find the decorations? Oh, this is truly going to be a marvellous Christmas. I only wish Conrad would come to church with us but there's no use asking him. I've tried for years now to get him to go but he has always refused.'

Marnie beamed her happiness but she didn't say a word. In a twinkling she was back with her presents and after loading her arms with Eva's off they went downstairs. Conrad saw them coming and immediately relieved Marnie of her burden and after catching and understanding Marnie's warning look said nothing to his grandmother about the tree. When they got to the door of the lounge he balanced the gifts on his knee while he flung open the door. The room was in total darkness except for the lights shining from the tree. It was a truly magnificent spectacle and both Marnie and Conrad watched while Eva stared at the tree, her beautiful worn face glowing from the Christmas tree lights and from her own light which glowed from within.

Eva moved slowly towards the tree, her eyes lifted to

the star. 'Grandfather's star!' she whispered brokenly, tears of happiness rolling down her cheeks. 'Grandfather's star!' she exclaimed again as though trying to convince herself that it was truly there.

Conrad stood beside Eva and together they looked at the star and Marnie knew their heads and hearts were filled with memories both good and bad, happy and sad. Strangely, she didn't feel left out, in fact she felt included because she had touched and held the star close to her breast and it was almost as if it had become a part of her . . . a part of her love and hope.

The gifts were put around the tree and Conrad looked curiously at the rather awkward shape of one of them. He reached down and picked it up, reading the little tag. He turned to Marnie, an amused expression on his face.

'This is for me?' He felt it, black brows arched inquisitively as he tried to figure what it could possibly be. Marnie rushed over and took it away from him.

'You're like a little boy,' she pretended to scold him, loving the male dimples creasing his cheeks. He grinned and his teeth flashed white against the darkness of his deep tan.

'I think I know what it is,' he teased her, a wicked glint in his eyes.

'Well, I'm not surprised,' she pretended to fume, 'you've practically unwrapped it.' When he reached for it again she slapped his hand very lightly and held it behind her back. 'Behave yourself,' she said in her best teacher's voice, 'or I will give it to someone who is a little more deserving.'

Eva chuckled beside them, her tired old eyes bright and warm as she looked lovingly from one to the other. 'Oh, this is the way Christmas should be!' she exclaimed happily. 'Lots of good old-fashioned fun!'

A deep throated chuckle poured from Conrad's

throat and the sound filled Marnie and Eva with delight, cloaking them in velvet. His arms slipped around their shoulders and he drew them close. Marnie couldn't remember a time she had felt so happy.

Several minutes later they managed to drag themselves from the tree. They arrived at the little church in Palm Beach with only seconds to spare before the first carol was sung.

The church was beautiful. Candles provided the only light and the children's choir were dressed in red, the adults in white. Palm trees rustled against the open windows and the gentle lapping of the surf provided the music whenever the organ didn't. We make a pretty good trio Marnie thought as she listened to their voices. Conrad's rich baritone, Eva's low alto and her own soprano. Their voices were lifted together as the beautiful carols took on a new meaning for her. She vowed she would never forget this evening.

Eva was very tired by the time they arrived back at the estate. Conrad carried her upstairs, Marnie beside him. Conrad stopped half-way up the stairs and looked down into his grandmother's face. Her eyes were closed. 'She's asleep,' he whispered softly to Marnie and Marnie nodded, although she knew Eva wasn't. She was only resting her eyes, something she did several times a day. Marnie took a deep breath and whispered softly back, knowing that Eva was listening.

'She's beautiful, isn't she?'

Conrad hugged Eva even closer against the strong wall of his chest. 'That she is,' he agreed soberly, his black eyes filled with tenderness as he gazed into the worn old face. A barely perceptible smile appeared on Eva's lips.

'You love her, don't you?' Marnie asked softly.

'Love her!' There was a fierceness in Conrad's voice. 'She's everything to me. My life as a child would have been sheer hell without her!' He gathered Eva even closer against him and Marnie watched as the smile on Eva's lips deepened and her features relaxed into the peaceful tranquillity. Her eyelids became still and Marnie knew that Eva was sleeping.

Conrad carried her into her bedroom and laid her gently down on the bed. 'Can you manage?' he asked Marnie in a low voice.

'Yes, I'll only remove what's necessary. I don't want to waken her.' She followed him to the door. He seemed reluctant to leave, his eyes caressing her face. His hand reached up to lightly stroke the soft curve of her cheek.

'It's Christmas,' he said, his eyes lingering on her mouth.

'Yes,' she agreed, her lips parting.

He bent his head and kissed her, his arms circling her in a protective embrace. Marnie clung to him, every tiny nerve in her body responding to his touch. At last he raised his head and smiled down into her flushed face.

'Merry Christmas, Marnie,' he said, punctuating each word with a kiss.

'Merry Christmas,' she husked softly, her lips trembling against his.

Neither was willing to let the other go but they didn't speak of their feelings. Marnie wondered what his reaction would be if she suddenly blurted out that she loved him. Would he be horrified? On the defensive? Amused? Would he say, 'Sorry, kid, but I'm already spoken for. However, it's nice, these little kisses we manage to sneak when no one is looking'?

He set her finally away from him. 'Get to bed as soon as you can, Marnie,' he suggested caringly. 'It's late and you look tired.'

'I am,' she admitted weakly, feeling suddenly cold now that she was no longer in his arms. Her expression brightened. 'I'll have to be up early to cook the turkey.'

His chuckle warmed her, reviving her flagging spirits. 'You sound as though you're actually looking forward to spending a day in the kitchen.'

'Yes, I am,' she admitted truthfully, hoping he would offer to help her. Not that she needed help, of course. It was just that it would be very pleasant to have his company. Very pleasant!

'Well, promise me you won't overdo things,' he said, bending his head to plant a kiss on the tip of her pert little nose. 'I wouldn't want anyone to think I've been taking advantage of your talents!'

He stepped into the hallway. 'What *is* that thing you've wrapped up for me?' he asked, amusement lighting his eyes.

'You'll find out soon enough,' she answered flippantly, tossing her head back to look at him through teasing eyes.

An enigmatic gleam shone from his eyes as he said in a softly warning growl. 'I could *make* you tell me!' Marnie's pulses raced at the all too obvious meaning behind his words. Her hands clutched at the door knob in an effort to steady herself.

'But then you wouldn't have anything to look forward to in the morning,' she answered in an amazingly calm voice, ignoring the blatantly suggestive remark.

He looked at her steadily for a long moment. 'Oh, yes, I would,' he assured her softly, bringing even more colour to her cheeks. 'Good night, Marnie.' He turned and walked down the hall.

'Good night, Conrad,' she whispered to his retreating back, before she softly closed the door.

Marnie thought she wouldn't sleep that night after the exciting events of the evening but as soon as her head touched the pillow she was off in dreamland. Her happiness hadn't left her during the night and she awoke with the same sort of expectancy she could remember having as a small child on Christmas morning. She leapt out of bed and after a quick shower, dressed into a pair of turquoise slacks and a white halter-type blouse.

When she stepped into the hallway Conrad was making his way towards her room with Eva on one side of his broad frame and Helena on the other. Eva was bright and greeted Marnie warmly, commenting about the Christmas presents under the tree which were waiting to be opened. Helena looked tired and was obviously suffering from a hangover, her make-up appearing dry and flakey on her face. She was dressed in a red frock which clashed with her orange lipstick. Marnie was amazed. Helena usually took such pains with her appearance.

Conrad was happy, Marnie saw immediately. Despite the lateness of their evening before he looked as rested as if he had just put in twelve hours of good solid sleep. Dressed in a yellow golf shirt and yellow shorts he looked the picture of health. Marnie smiled at all three. Two returned her smile, Helena merely glared at her.

Conrad put his finger to his mouth. 'Quiet, please. If we want to open our presents without an audience then we had better get away from here as quickly and as quietly as possible.'

They tiptoed past the bedrooms where the guests were sleeping and made their way downstairs.

Helena didn't comment on the tree, but then Marnie didn't really expect her to. She was amazed that Helena had even bothered to come downstairs with them and she wondered if Conrad had wakened her for this purpose. Then Marnie managed to get a grip on herself. Helena was Conrad's special guest, his lady. Marnie, despite her fantasies, was merely his grandmother's temporary companion.

Conrad handed out the gifts, giving Eva the first one. It was from Marnie. A leather bound volume of verses by Byron, Eva's favourite poet. Eva clasped it to her and tears sprang to her eyes at the inscription inside: 'To Eva, a very gentle lady'.

'Thank you, Marnie, this is truly lovely,' Eva managed to say, wiping her eyes with her lace handkerchief.

Conrad handed a gift to Helena. Helena opened it with little interest. Eva leaned forward and then Marnie recognised the wrapping. It was the beautiful diamond pendant Eva had worried over. Helena took it out and the early morning sun caught and turned the diamonds into blazing globes. Helena yawned and put it back into its little case.

'That's the same gift you gave me last year, Eva,' she drawled in forced amusement. 'Really, dear, your memory is slipping badly.' She raised her head to Conrad. 'You should see about this, darling,' she pretended to be anxious. 'Lapses of memory can be dangerous you know.'

Conrad's eyes were glittering with a cold contempt as he looked down at Helena. His lips were compressed into a hard, tight line and Marnie could sense Eva becoming nervous by her side. Always the one to maintain a peaceful harmony, Eva quickly said: 'Is it, Helena? Oh dear, you could be right. I'll take it back . . . get you something else. Perhaps a nice sweater?'

Helena picked up the discarded box and slipped it into the pocket of her dress. 'Don't be silly, darling,' she said quickly. 'I wouldn't *dream* of putting you to all that extra bother.'

Conrad held out his hand. 'Give me the box, Helena,' he ordered in a deadly quiet voice. Helena hesitated for only a fraction of a second before she took the box from her pocket and reluctantly handed it to him. He flicked the lid open and stared down at the beautiful pendant. At last he looked over at Eva and then crossed to where she was sitting. He handed her the box. 'It's truly a superb piece of craftsmanship,' he said tightly, 'and it's original.' His eyes moved to Marnie's and she saw that at last he was starting to realise that Helena wasn't all that he believed her to be.

Eva sat with the box in her hand not knowing what to do with it. Helena sat staring at the box, licking her lips. Marnie was filled with disgust and it was all she could do to remain in the room. Finally, Eva placed the box with its expensive treasure on a small table beside her where Helena barely took her eyes from it. Marnie wondered if the girl had at last learned a lesson.

Despite that little episode, the rest of the gift giving was a happy and somewhat amusing event. It was largely due to Conrad's determination that the morning went so well and Marnie knew he wanted this Christmas to be happy in every way for Eva.

Conrad's gift to his grandmother was a silk scarf and a pair of kid gloves for winter. Similar to what she gave him and they joked about this. He handed a gift to Marnie and she unwrapped it with trembling fingers and a glowing heart. She hadn't expected him to give her anything so the gift was all the more pleasant on account of it. It was an enormous bottle of hollyhock bubble bath! Marnie put her hand to her mouth to suppress the laughter which threatened to tumble from her throat.

She felt his eyes on her but she dared not look at him because Helena's eyes were also on her and she felt the hostility radiating from those hard, green orbs. Helena would surely be wondering at his choice of gift, she knew.

Conrad left the bulky present which he knew to be from Marnie to the last. He stood staring down at it, his chin in his hand as he quietly contemplated it. Finally he bent and picked it up, carefully unwrapping it. It was a surfboard. A yellow plastic surfboat suitable for a child. His black eyes swept over to Marnie and they were filled with delight. In his hand was the little card and on it was written: 'In memory of all those bruises . . .!'

'What ridiculous gifts!' Helena snapped from where she was sitting, holding her pile of gifts. Her eyes blazed angrily from Conrad to Marnie. 'Bubble bath and a surfboard. Thank heavens you didn't see fit to play jokes like that on *me*!'

'Jokes are only for the pure of heart,' Conrad offered casually and Helena frowned, not quite understanding what he meant.

The wrapping paper was collected and put in a spare box by Marnie and Conrad. Eva and Helena had gone back upstairs, Eva to read and Helena to sleep.

'I've got some paper work to attend to in my study,' Conrad said, 'otherwise I would take out my new surfboard and see how it goes.' His eyes were shining.

'Must you work on Christmas Day?' Marnie asked him softly. 'You deserve a break just like anyone else.'

He smiled down at her. 'I can't afford to let the paper work mount up.' His hand reached out to gently stroke her cheek. 'What are you going to do?'

'I'll be busy as well,' she said. 'What's Christmas without a turkey? I've got to get "old Tom" ready for the oven.'

'Ah,' he exclaimed with obvious satisfaction. 'I'd forgotten about "old Tom". I'll leave my study door open so I can catch the first tantalising aroma!'

'Well, you won't get that for quite some time,' she chuckled, loving the feel of his hand on her skin. 'Do you want me to make you some breakfast?'

He shook his head. 'No, Flora will have that on the

table soon enough. It's the turkey I want you to spend your time on.' His eyes gleamed down at her. 'Did you like your bubble bath?'

Colour stained her cheeks. 'You know I did.' And then, 'I ... I wonder what Helena and ... and Eva thought?' she asked in a faintly anxious tone.

He smiled down at her. 'Grandmother would have thought it was a nice, practical gift and Helena would have thought it was an inexpensive one.'

But it wasn't. The brand name and the size revealed it was bubbly gold! 'Yes, I suppose you're right,' Marnie sighed with relief. There would be no questions, therefore no explanations would be required.

'Will I see you at breakfast?' he asked, his eyes travelling over her face.

'No, I expect I'll be busy and I'll probably reek of onions,' she laughed. 'I'll grab something in the kitchen.'

'Make certain you do,' he warned. He bent his head and kissed her. She was going to the kitchen and he was off to his study, but they were reluctant to part. They may as well have been travelling to different corners of the world. At last he let her go, turning her around and giving her a little pat on her bottom. 'Off with you, woman!' he growled.

Marnie's feet had wings on them as she made her way to the kitchen. Flora and Annie were preparing breakfast and neither turned when Marnie entered nor did they respond to her cheery 'Merry Christmas'. But Marnie barely noticed. She was standing in front of the opened refrigerator, her eyes wide with puzzlement.

The turkeys which she had placed in there herself were no longer there! Old Tom Turkey had gone missing!

CHAPTER NINE

'I think I'll make myself a cup of coffee,' Conrad announced as he came into the kitchen. He stopped short at the sight of Marnie peering into the refrigerator. He came over and stood beside her, peering in as well. 'What are we looking for?' he asked after a while, amusement threading through the deep tones of his voice.

'The turkeys,' Marnie answered, looking up at him. 'They've gone!' There was an edge of disbelief to her voice and a silent sort of pleading look to her eyes that begged him to find them for her. They both turned back to peer once more into the refrigerator, Marnie reaching in to move things around on the shelf, as though somehow the two large turkeys might be hiding behind a pound of butter.

'Well, they sure as hell aren't in here!' Conrad remarked, closing the door. His eyes swung over to where Flora and Annie were busy preparing breakfast for the guests.

'Have either of you seen the turkeys?' he demanded to know.

Flora turned slowly around, trying to mask the sullen expression she usually wore on her face as she squared up to her employer. 'Have you checked the freezer?' she asked, wiping her hands on her apron.

'The freezer!' Marnie moaned. 'Oh, no they can't be! I can't stuff a *frozen* turkey!'

But when Conrad opened the freezer door there they were, frozen solid. He lifted them out and carried them across to the table, placing each one down with a loud, hard thump. Anger welled up in Marnie's throat as she stared down at the turkeys.

'Who ... who put them in the freezer?' she asked stiffly, trying desperately hard to keep her anger from showing.

Flora shrugged. 'Could have been anyone,' she offered casually. 'People have been in and out of the fridge ever since the guests arrived. Maybe someone wanted to make some room for beer or something. After all, they did take up an awful lot of space.'

'And the ham?' Marnie enquired. 'Is the ham in the freezer as well?'

'The ham?' Flora's eyes widened in surprise. 'The ham is almost gone!' she said. 'I've been using it for cold cuts and sandwiches. I've already fried up a big portion for this morning's breakfast. I thought that was what it was for.'

'Well, it wasn't,' Marnie said, a painful lump in the back of her throat causing the words to sound constricted. She swallowed hard, but the lump refused to budge and to her horror she felt tears pricking behind her eyelids. There was no doubt in her mind that Helena was behind this sabotage, that she had set out to deliberately destroy any chances Marnie might have had in making this a grand occasion.

Conrad was watching her, aware of her distress. He put a comforting arm around her shoulders. 'They can be cooked frozen, can't they?' he enquired softly, his tone encouraging.

No, but there was the microwave. If she put them in there on 'defrost' not too much time would be wasted.

She looked up at him. 'No, there's the risk of food poisoning cooking meat from frozen,' she said, aware of Flora's eyes on them and the fact that Conrad's arm was around her shoulders. She knew this would be relayed to Helena and that when it was Helena would sharpen her claws! 'But I can defrost them in the microwave you brought down from Eva's room.'

Apart from periodically checking on Eva, Marnie worked the whole day on the Christmas dinner. She prepared the stuffing while the turkeys were defrosting. Her stuffing was her own secret recipe and consisted of sausage, apples, prunes, raisins, dates and onions and a whole loaf of crispy bread. She chopped, diced, peeled and sliced until her fingers felt like limp strands of spaghetti. Then she stuffed the turkeys and put them in the oven. The giblets she put to simmer, ready for making the gravy.

Flora and Annie watched her curiously and to Marnie's astonishment even made her a cup of tea and a sandwich at lunch time. Several times while Marnie was tending to Eva she would return to the kitchen to find one or the other basting the turkeys for her. During the day a sort of companionship developed between them. Pretty soon the house was filled with the tantalising aroma of the turkeys and several times Conrad came into the kitchen to check on their progress. So did a lot of the guests, mainly Conrad's guests, whom Marnie quite liked. They were mostly young married couples in the same line of work as Conrad. Helena stayed away, resting up for the evening ahead.

In the late afternoon Marnie set the table in the dining room. Counting herself and Eva there would be twenty-four at the table, as some of the neighbours were joining them. She used the best of everything: the best linen table cloth, the finest china and cutlery, with the Wright family emblem inscribed on each piece. The gardener directed her to the part of the garden where the finest blooms were ready to be picked and she made a centrepiece with flowers chosen for their colour which best suited the occasion and the decor of the room.

At last all was ready and she stood back to admire

the room which had been thoroughly vacuumed and polished with not a speck of dust to be found anywhere. The long table was the epitome in elegance, the silverware, crockery and glasses sparkling under the soft lighting from the overhead chandelier.

Her chest swelled with pride at what she had managed to achieve. Conrad and Eva would have the Christmas dinner they had missed out on for so many years.

With a final check on the turkeys, the gravy and the vegetables, Marnie finally went upstairs to get herself and Eva ready for dinner. She got Eva ready first. They had already decided on what Eva was to wear and she had had her bath, so it was only a matter of helping her into the pale pink silk frock and applying a spot of make-up before she was ready.

Back in her own room Marnie drew herself a bath, putting in a liberal amount of hollyhock bubble bath before easing her tired body into the foaming, sweet-scented water. She soaked until all her muscles were relaxed, but her mind was whirling over small details she might have forgotten over the meal. At last she stepped out of the tub and wrapped herself in a fluffy pink towel and padded into the bedroom.

She took her time in dressing. Her white chiffon dress was one of her favourite frocks and had only been worn once before. She slipped it on and stood in front of the mirror. Her golden tan and dark hair suited the dress to perfection.

After applying a thin layer of make-up, paying special attention to her eyes, she knew she had never looked better. There was a glow to her skin and eyes that she had never noticed before and her cheeks were flushed with excitement. Slipping into a pair of white high-heeled sandals she again looked at the woman in the mirror.

Her image shone back at her. High cheekbones in a perfect oval, eyes bright as any star. The dainty bones of her shoulders glistened under her smooth tan. She was delicate and fragile looking but she was far from thin. Satisfied that she could do no more to improve her appearance she slipped from her room to make one final check of the table and the meal.

Marnie went to the kitchen first. The serving bowls were in the warming oven ready to be laden with the vegetables. Two platters were resting on the kitchen table ready for the turkeys. Satisfied that everything was under control in the kitchen Marnie made her way to the dining room.

The room looked beautiful. She stepped over to straighten a sprig of fern in the centrepiece and adjusted a knife here, a fork there. She stood back again, allowing her eyes to roam freely over the table Her brow suddenly puckered. Unconsciously she had counted the place settings and now she counted them again, this time with a conscious effort.

Twenty-two! She counted again to make sure. Somebody had removed two of the settings. The table was now set for twenty-two people instead of twenty-four! Marnie sighed and shook her head. It had to be Helena of course. While Marnie was upstairs getting ready Helena must have slipped down and removed two places at the table. Marnie's and Eva's.

Marnie could visualise what would have happened had they all poured into the dining room. Two people would have been left standing and Eva being the kind of person she was would have insisted one of the guests take her place and then Marnie being Eva's companion would have naturally offered her place as well. Confusion and bedlam would have broken out. Conrad would have insisted that two extra places be set but the whole mood of the meal would have been destroyed by

that time. Each person at the table would have thought
it was their place which had been forgotten, and
Conrad would have most surely thought she was to
blame.

Poor Helena, Marnie thought, as she quickly
rearranged the settings to make room for two more, she
just never gives up. Marnie stayed in the dining room as
long as she dared before she raced back upstairs to
collect Eva. If Helena had any more plans up her sleeve
she was too late to put them into practice. The guests
were already starting to come out from their bedrooms
and make their way to the lounge for pre-dinner drinks.

Conrad came out of his bedroom looking superbly
handsome in a white dinner suit and black tie which he
was trying to knot.

'Would you like me to help you with that?' Marnie
asked, laughing at the look of agitation he was
displaying as he wrestled with the tie.

'Would I?' He dropped his hands to his side and
leaned towards her. 'Be my guest.'

Marnie expertly knotted it and stood back from him.
His eyes swept over her and she saw the naked
appreciation in those glittering black vessels.

'You look beautiful, Marnie,' he said huskily, making
her feel warm and bubbly inside. 'Every male in the
house will have his eyes on you,' he growled, not
sounding very pleased at the prospect.

Marnie didn't comment, feeling suddenly very shy
and unsure of herself. Why should he care who paid her
any attention? Helena was his concern, not herself.

He put his hands up to his tie. 'Who taught you to do
this?' His eyes narrowed, searching her face. 'A
boyfriend?'

Marnie's lips curved into a smile. 'My mother, so I
could tie father's if she happened to be out or busy.'

She was puzzled by his relief. It was such a small

thing to be concerned about but he had obviously been concerned that she was in the practice of performing small favours for boyfriends. Men! she thought, amazed again at how insecure most of them were at times.

'Is grandmother ready?' he asked.

'Yes.'

'Good. I'll escort her downstairs.'

'Oh, she will love that!' Marnie exclaimed, her violet coloured eyes shining. 'I'll just make sure that she's ready to come downstairs.' And she hurried off. It wouldn't do to keep the host from his guests. As Marnie reached Eva's door, Helena stepped out of her own bedroom.

Marnie froze with her hand on the door knob. Helena looked stunning, and suddenly Marnie felt like an untried school girl in comparison. Helena was dressed in a black low-cut evening gown, the fabric of the dress following every seductive curve in her body. Her hair was brushed loosely about her head, falling in soft waves across silky white shoulders. Make-up had been applied expertly and Marnie realised as she watched Helena sweep past her without even so much as a glance, that Helena could have been a movie star.

She watched the door open and stepped into Eva's room, not having the courage to witness Conrad's reaction as Helena made her way to him. Inside the room, Marnie leaned against the door feeling physically ill. She could picture Conrad and Helena right now. Two beautiful people admiring each other, looking into the other's eyes. Were they kissing right now? She almost opened the door to check. Her heart was thudding wildly in her chest and her stomach felt as though it had received a fatal blow.

I'm jealous! she thought wildly, hating herself for this feeling but seemingly helpless against it. She pressed her knuckles to her mouth and squeezed her eyes shut. All along I've been jealous! Had it shown? Did Conrad know she was jealous of Helena? Was that why he never believed Helena could do anything wrong because he felt Marnie was making jealous accusations?

Accusations based on jealousy. Oh my God, she thought desperately, sagging against the door. How can I possibly go through the evening with Conrad thinking what he must? Thank goodness she hadn't mentioned to him about the place settings. It would only have been her word against Helena's and now that the table had been restored what proof did she really have that the table had been tampered with in the first place?

Eva came out of her dressing room, wringing her hands in despair. Marnie gathered herself together and moved slowly away from the door and towards Eva.

'What's wrong, Eva?' she asked in a voice which didn't sound like her own.

Eva sat on the edge of her bed and looked up at Marnie with stricken eyes. 'The diamond pendant!' she whispered hoarsely. 'It's gone!'

'Gone?' Marnie echoed. 'What are you talking about?'

'The pendant I gave Helena. I got to thinking about Conrad taking it back from her and it didn't seem fair. I thought she might like to wear it this evening but when I looked for it, it was gone.'

Marnie tried to think. 'You put it on the table beside the chair you were sitting on downstairs in the lounge. Perhaps it got knocked off and rolled under the chair.'

'I looked under the chair. I even took off the cushions and looked there as well. Then I thought perhaps I'd taken it up here with me but when I went through everything it was nowhere to be found.'

Marnie sat down on the bed beside her. 'I'm trying to think if it was still on the table when Conrad and I tidied up.' She shook her head. 'I really can't remember, but it must have been. Oh dear, you don't suppose it might have been knocked to the floor and was accidentally picked up with all the wrapping paper?' Then Marnie shook her head. 'No, it was in its box,' she answered her own question. 'We would have felt it through the flimsy paper.'

'Then what do you suppose happened to it?' Eva asked, her eyes wide. 'You don't . . . you don't think somebody has . . . has stolen it?' She clasped the sides of her face with her hands. 'Oh, dear, what a perfectly terrible thing for me to think, never mind say!'

'Have you said anything about this to anyone?' Marnie asked.

'No, nothing, not a word. I've been too busy looking for it and far too worried. I just can't imagine anyone taking it but . . . but . . .'

'But the possibility is there.' Marnie finished the sentence for her. She stood up and reached for Eva's hands. 'Conrad is waiting to escort you downstairs,' she smiled gently. 'I don't want you worrying over the pendant tonight, I want you to enjoy the evening. We'll look for it tomorrow and I'm sure we'll find it. In the meantime, well, I think it would be better if we kept this to ourselves until we've made a thorough search. If we don't find it then naturally Conrad will have to be informed.'

There was a knock on the door and Conrad appeared. 'What's the hold-up?' he asked, stepping inside.

'I'm not quite ready yet,' Eva told him, sounding flustered. 'You go on ahead dear and Marnie and I will catch up in a few minutes.'

His smile touched them both. 'Nonsense. You look fine and you're obviously ready. I think you've got a classic case of cold feet.' A few easy strides and he was standing in front of them. 'Come on, ladies, off we go. A sherry will help to ease your nerves.'

This time it was Marnie who cast Eva a warning glance. Eva understood and smiled up at her grandson. 'My, but you do look handsome tonight,' she said in a genuinely proud voice. She slipped her frail arm into his big strong one and he gently patted her hand.

'And you,' he said with the same pride, 'look especially beautiful tonight.' His eyes moved over to Marnie. 'You both do!'

Had he said the same thing to Helena? Marnie wondered, and then immediately felt ashamed of herself. He would have to be blind not to notice Helena's beauty and Conrad wasn't blind!

The guests had already assembled in the lounge by the time they arrived to join in on the festivities. Most were standing in front of the tree openly admiring it. Marnie had hung back so that no one would get the mistaken impression that she was trying to take any of the limelight from Eva, or that she held herself in more importance than the companion she had been hired to be.

However, she was reluctantly drawn in when Conrad turned to her and said, reaching for her hand. 'It appears our tree is the centre of attention and judging from the comments the finest anyone has seen.'

Marnie drew her hand from his, hoping no one had noticed. Her eyes swept over to Helena and she realised with a sinking heart that the gesture hadn't gone unobserved. She wondered what Helena would do to retaliate.

Conrad led his grandmother to the same chair she had been sitting on that morning and while he fetched them both a sherry Marnie's eyes wandered to the floor in search of the pendant. She wished she could have a good look under the chair, but of course she couldn't do that. But she certainly would in the morning. After all, Eva's eyesight wasn't very sharp and she could have missed seeing it against the patterned rug.

Marnie noticed that most of Helena's guests had all but departed, leaving mainly Conrad's There was such a stark contrast between the two groups. Helena's friends were 'way out' dressers while Conrad's friends seemed rather plain in comparison. Helena's friends seemed to find everything hilariously funny while Conrad's friends laughed quietly. But as different as the two groups were, Marnie couldn't imagine any one of them as being a thief.

Conrad's friends were obviously wealthy and while that didn't disqualify them from stealing they just weren't the type. And Helena's friends wore plenty of jewellery, but their taste bordered on the gaudy. The diamond pendant Eva had given Helena was a classical piece and wouldn't hold much interest to any one of them. No, it was hard to imagine anyone in this room as a thief. Perhaps the pendant had got mixed up with the wrapping paper. The more Marnie considered this possibility the more likely it seemed. She would check on that in the morning as well.

Conrad returned with their drinks. He handed one to his grandmother and the other to Marnie. When Marnie took hers, her hand accidentally brushed against his, sending a wild shiver racing up her arm. Conrad's black eyes gleamed down at her and Marnie lowered her eyes, detesting the amused mockery she had seen in them, making her realise he was well aware of the havoc he could play on her senses.

The hour passed very pleasantly with easy chatter and soft laughter, occasionally interrupted by the arrival of more guests. Music played in the background and small groups gathered around Eva and Marnie. Eva's cheeks were pink with excitement over all the attention she was receiving. Conrad stayed mostly with Marnie and Eva, moving away only to refill the occasional glass, greet the new arrivals, and twice to talk with Helena who had chosen for reasons of her own to remain away from them. Several times Marnie felt Helena's cold green eyes on her and when she looked up there was always that naked look of gloating triumph in them. Marnie found she couldn't keep herself from smiling. She must remember to watch Helena's face when they entered the dining room to find that there were twenty-four place settings!

Marnie excused herself to check on the progress in the kitchen. Flora and Annie had changed into fresh serving dresses for the occasion and despite their friendliness, which had developed during the day spent in the kitchen, Marnie found she was still distrustful of them and she knew this feeling was prompted by Helena's final attempt to sabotage the dinner. Besides, Marnie hadn't forgotten the conversation in the kitchen which she had overhead.

'I think we had better start to serve now,' Marnie told them, 'otherwise the turkeys will be dry. I'll inform Conrad to make the announcement to the guests. I imagine ten minutes will see us sitting at the table.'

Flora took out a large carving knife and advanced towards the turkeys.

'Flora!' Marnie gasped as Flora wielded the knife over the turkey. 'What are you doing?'

'Carving them,' Flora announced in surprise. 'You said you want to serve them. It will take me at least the ten minutes to get . . .'

Marnie rushed over and shoved the turkeys out of Flora's reach. 'Conrad will carve. Everyone must see how lovely they look. That's half the glory of a Christmas dinner, seeing a big, crispy brown turkey!'

Flora's eyes narrowed on Marnie. 'I think it's the glory you want for yourself, not for these here birds. I suppose you've been telling everyone that you cooked the dinner?'

'I think everyone realises it already,' Marnie answered quietly. 'After all, most of them came into the kitchen today and if you remember some of the guests even helped prepare the vegetables. Now if you will excuse me I think I will just carry this in myself,' said Marnie as she lifted one heavy platter. 'By the time you get the vegetables into their serving dishes we should be at the table. Annie, make certain there are two gravy boats on the table. Put one at either end. And bring the other turkey.' With that Marnie marched from the kitchen carrrying her precious cargo along with the realisation she had only just managed to rescue the turkeys from being hacked up and served to the guests with as little aplomb as a plate of cold cuts. Like the ham, she thought, still bristling.

Marnie placed her platter at the end of the table in front of where Conrad would be sitting. Just to reassure herself, she quickly counted the places at the table. Still twenty-four.

When she got back to the lounge, Conrad was standing in a far corner of the room talking with Helena. Marnie noticed this right away because as always her eyes were drawn to him like a magnet and there really was nothing she could do about it.

Helena was being extremely animated, her hands moving wildly as she expressed herself. Conrad burst into a loud boom of laughter while Helena's giggles floated across the room. Conrad looked up and seeing Marnie said something to Helena and crossed over to where she stood by Eva's chair. Helena watched him go with obvious disapproval and then turned to one of her male friends.

'Where did you disappear to?' Conrad asked immediately, his dark eyes smiling down at her. 'To check on things in the kitchen, I'll wager.'

'Yes,' Marnie answered, aware of the breathless

quality in her voice. 'Everything is ready. You had better announce that dinner will now be served,' she finished grandly, her eyes sparkling up at him.

He chuckled and pressed the back of his hand against her cheek. 'Your face is hot. I hope you haven't overdone things. I warned you not to.'

'I feel fine,' she answered a little untruthfully, for actually she was deliriously happy. He only had to touch her and her whole being responded like a symphony bursting into life.

'I think I know how you're feeling,' he bent his head to say quietly, and for a brief second as Marnie looked into his eyes she felt . . . no she knew, he felt the same way. But the look was gone, or carefully concealed, she didn't know which, before she could guarantee for herself that it actually had been there.

They formed a procession and marched to the tune of the Drummer Boy into the dining room, with Eva on Conrad's arm and leading the way. Marnie saw a wicked gleam shine in Helena's eyes as the guests circled the table to stand behind their chairs. Helena's eyes widened in astonishment and then blazed with anger when each guest, including Eva and Marnie, was standing behind a chair. Her eyes darted menacingly over at Marnie and Marnie met her look with an innocent smile, trying hard not to look like the cat who had swallowed the cream.

Conrad was in exceptionally good spirits and actually managed to sound boastful as he drew everyone's attention to the fact that Marnie had planned and, with only a minimal amount of help, had cooked, a grand meal for so many people. He raised his glass in a toast and Marnie blushed scarlet as glasses were raised and voices around the table saluted her.

Next he toasted his grandmother and his eyes shone with pride as Eva acknowledged her toast, looking as

elegant and as grand as any queen. Someone stood up
and toasted the turkeys, and by the time Conrad picked
up the carving knife to begin serving everyone was
having a marvellous time.

The meal was everything Marnie had hoped it would
be. Conrad had chosen the right wines and the turkey
was succulent, the vegetables weren't over-cooked and
as she had promised him, there were no lumps in the
gravy. There were several pleas for the recipe of the
stuffing, but she teasingly refused to divulge her secret.
By the time the meal was over Marnie had become the
most celebrated 'guest'. At the end of the main course,
she was toasted again, and they all declared that a good
old-fashioned Christmas dinner was much nicer by far
than a barbecue. Throughout all this Helena sat in
silent wrath.

Conrad had suggested they have dessert on the patio
and tables had been set for this. The soft breeze, the
moonlight, the heady fragrance of frangipani blossoms
and the music blending in with the roll of the surf
added romance to the evening. The Christmas pudding
was wheeled out on a trolley and Conrad poured
brandy over it and struck a match to it. Flames lit up
the centre of the table and once again applause broke
out. It was just one of those evenings when everyone
(well almost everyone) felt wonderfully alive and happy
and they wanted to show it. Coffee was served with the
appropriate liqueurs and everyone settled back in easy
comaraderie.

'Conrad,' Helena said in a falsely worried tone.
'Don't you think your grandmother looks tired?'
Without waiting for his answer, Helena turned to
Marnie. 'I think it's about time you took her up to bed.'

There was abrupt silence. Marnie felt her backbone
stiffening. Helena's choice of words had completely
destroyed Eva's independent image, the grand lady of

the household. With one blow Helena had successfully taken the wind from Eva's sails. Visibly, Eva began to sag and a tremulous smile worked its way around her mouth. She started to get up from her chair, embarrassed that she had overstayed her welcome.

'Yes, I am tired,' she said in a weary voice. 'I don't expect you young people want an old lady around.' She attempted a laugh. 'It must be like having a chaperone!'

'Nonsense!' Conrad's voice sounded like a whip cracking. 'You stay up much later than this, Grandmother. You can sleep in in the morning, although knowing you I doubt that would be possible.'

Eva smiled warmly across at him. Several others interjected as well, begging Eva to stay. She sat back in her chair, her eyes glistening. 'Well, I suppose it wouldn't hurt to stay a bit longer,' she allowed herself to be coaxed.

A young man whom Marnie had sat next to during the meal suddenly turned to her, snapping his fingers. 'Hamilton! Your father doesn't happen to lecture at the Sydney University does he? Philosophy?'

'Why, yes,' Marnie admitted. The awkward moment caused by Helena had passed and Marnie was once more relaxed. 'Or at least he used to, but he's retired now.'

'Marvellous man,' the young fellow continued. 'Brilliant scholar. Had him as a lecturer during my final year there. Couldn't have made it without his help.' His eyes moved appraisingly over Marnie's features. 'Fancy him having a beautiful daughter like you!' he exclaimed to everyone's delight.

Marnie chuckled good-naturedly and reached over to place her coffee cup on the table. As she leaned back again in her chair she was aware of Conrad's eyes on her and she realised with a sudden jolt that he had taken offence at the young man's innocent compliment to her. A muscle jerked spasmodically alongside his jaw as he glowered across at her. He placed his cup alongside hers and stood up.

'It's getting rather chilly out here,' he announced. 'Let's move inside, shall we?'

Why, of all the pompous, overbearing actions! Marnie quietly fumed as she watched the guests all stand up to abide by his ruling. He helped Eva from her chair and led her inside with Marnie reluctantly following. It was a beautiful evening, not at all chilly and the prospect of having to sit in the lounge with cigarette smoke billowing around her wasn't at all inviting, after the purity of the fresh evening air.

Marnie sensed that Eva had indeed had enough. The move from the patio to the lounge had taken the zip from the party and tiredness crept up on her as well.

'Conrad,' she said in a soft voice just before they were to sit down again, 'I'm feeling rather tired.' She looked at Eva and saw that Eva was relieved. 'I think Eva and I will retire for the evening,' So formal, she thought. *Retire for the evening*! Why didn't she just say 'We've had it.' Or, 'We're exhausted. We're off to our rooms.' Suddenly her temples started to throb and she put her hands up to them.

'Are you all right?' Conrad asked in a worried frown.

'Y-Yes, just a slight headache, that's all.' She attempted a smile. 'Nothing to worry about.' She reached for Eva's arm but Conrad intervened.

'I'll help you upstairs, Grandmother,' he said, taking the arm Marnie had reached for. Eva smiled tenderly at them.

'My, my, all this attention! The two of you are spoiling me.' She turned to Marnie. 'Why don't you stay and enjoy the party, dear? I can make it up to my room without any help.' She turned to Conrad. 'You too, dear,' she said, removing her arm from his gentle grip. 'Please don't fuss so.'

But Marnie didn't want to stay downstairs. She knew Eva was tired and nothing would be gained by remaining at the party. Dance music was playing and several couples were already waltzing across the floor and moving towards the tiled patio. Helena was threading her way through the guests in their direction. She came up to Conrad and flung her arms around his neck.

'Dance?' she asked in a crooning voice.

While Conrad was removing Helena's arms from around his neck Marnie took Eva's arm and they quietly slipped away.

Upstairs in her room Marnie stood alone on her balcony. The party hadn't gone on as long as she had thought it might and now all was quiet. It was the moment she had been waiting for, and like she had done once before she slipped from her room and made her way to the beach. She had to be alone where she could think and try to unravel the mysteries of her heart.

The soft, balmy breeze tossed the skirt of her dress, the white chiffon billowing about her knees. She closed her eyes and lifted her face to the sky, drinking in deeply the sweet scented air. The waves rolled in, breaking against the shore, and the sound soothed her troubled spirit.

When she opened her eyes Conrad was standing in front of her, only a few paces away. He held his arms out to her and she walked towards them, pressing her cheek against his chest and putting her arms around his waist. His arms circled her in a warm embrace, holding her tightly against him.

'Marnie,' he murmured against her hair. 'Oh, Marnie, I've been waiting for you. I knew you would come.'

CHAPTER TEN

MARNIE looked up at him, her eyes glowing. 'You've been waiting for me?' she asked incredulously. The top button of his shirt was undone and his black tie hung loosely around his neck. He had been holding his dinner jacket, slung over one shoulder, but he had dropped it when he held out his arms to her. Now he bent down to retrieve it from the sand and after giving it a shake draped it around her shoulders.

Lifting her effortlessly, he carried her across the beach to the dunes and laid her down on his jacket, stretching out beside her. He gathered her close in his arms and stroked the soft curve of her cheek.

'Yes, you little imp,' he drawled huskily, finally answering her, 'I've been waiting for you. I've wanted to hold you in my arms all night.' He bent his head and kissed her, a gentle, loving kiss and one which made no demands on her.

Marnie snuggled against him, a feeling of peace invading her whole being. Neither spoke, each listening to the beat of the other's heart and to the soothing sound of the surf. The moon had dipped away and their only light was the stars sparkling above them. It was as if they were the only two people left in the world and the world was very peaceful.

Marnie opened her eyes to find the world on fire! The sky was bathed in crimson, red fingers streaking across the universe in multiple shades of scarlet tonings. The ocean was charged with shimmering shades of coral, rippling and splashing against the sandy beach, now the colour of fairy floss, all soft and sugary pink.

Daybreak! Marnie disentangled herself from Conrad's arms and sat up, marvelling at the beauty of the first dawning light, before turning to look down at the sleeping man beside her. Her lips curved into a loving smile at the picture he made. Totally relaxed in sleep he looked much younger than his thirty-odd years. Long, spiky black lashes curled against the tanned smoothness of his skin and the handsome line of his mouth had lost all its harshness. Black hair tumbled across his forehead, almost touching the fine lines of his brows. One hand was curled into a loose fist above his head, the other was in her lap.

She bent her head and kissed him. His eyes flew open, and she laughed at the startled innocence in them. His hand cupped her head and he didn't have to force her to kiss him again. The hand on her lap tightened around her thigh.

'Guess what?' she murmured against his lips. 'We slept on the beach. It's morning!'

'Is that why the sun is shining?' he asked, pretending surprise as he nibbled on her mouth.

'It is,' she agreed, allowing herself to be pulled across his chest, as his kisses grew in intensity. 'And you know what else?' she managed to ask between kisses.

'What?' he asked after several moments, his heart thumping under hers.

'We had better get ourselves up to the house . . . *fast!*'

He rolled her on to her back, his hands on either side of her as he looked deeply into her eyes. 'Why?' he growled.

She smiled up at him. 'Because if we don't, someone might get up and see us still dressed and know we haven't been to bed. They . . .' She swallowed hard, wishing he wouldn't look at her like that. 'They might get the wrong impression.'

He looked at her for a long while before he finally

said with a reluctant sigh. 'Yes, I suppose you're right. There would be some who would think the worst, I'm afraid.' He stood up and extended his hand. She placed her own small one into his and watched while his tanned fingers closed around it, completely covering it as he pulled her up beside him. His hand held hers while his other moved up to her face, one long finger gently tucking a silky strand of hair behind her ear. He bent his head and kissed the tip of her nose.

'You look beautiful in the morning, Marnie,' he told her huskily. 'All soft and rosy.'

The colour in the cheeks deepened. 'You do, too,' she answered shyly.

'What!' His brows were raised in mock horror. 'Soft and rosy?'

'That too,' she agreed teasingly, peeping up at him through the silky fringe of her lashes. 'But mostly, just beautiful.'

His deep throated chuckle washed over her like a cool, refreshing spring. A thrill of excitement raced up her spine when his hand tightened on her own. They turned as one towards the rolling surf and to watch the sunrise show off more of its colour. The sky looked orange now, the deep reds fading away into softer colours, with only the sudden streak of purple to remind them of what it had been like before. The surf had a light tinge of pink still on its caps, magnificent against the turquoise colour of the smoother waters.

'Isn't it beautiful?' Marnie sighed and then laughed in delight when a group of pelicans appeared as if from nowhere and swooped over them, their huge wings fanning the balmy morning air as they winged above them and then glided gracefully down into the ocean.

Seagulls joined them, competing for food. Some strutted in front of Marnie and Conrad. 'Sorry, old chaps,' Conrad apologised. 'Fresh out of tucker this morning.' He looked down at Marnie. 'Do you really want to get up to the house or shall we have a swim?'

Marnie didn't hesitate. 'The house,' she answered firmly.

Conrad grinned. 'I rather suspected that would be your choice. No skinny dipping for you, eh?' His grin deepened as she started to protest, but he only squeezed her hand again. 'Don't worry about it. I know you school teachers have an image to protect. After all, what if the pelicans or the seagulls *told* somebody?'

Laughter gurgled from Marnie's throat and her eyes were shining with delight. 'You're so right!' She gave a mournful sigh and looked across the waters. 'You just never know with pelicans. They can't be trusted.'

'It's the seagulls I worry about. Such a noisy, nosey lot!'

As if on cue a band of seagulls started an ear-shattering fight over a soldier crab which had just dug his way up through the warm sand. Marnie and Conrad turned and made their way towards the house. Everything was quiet and peaceful, curtains still drawn across bedroom windows. The gardens surrounding the beautiful house were glistening with early morning dew and the sweet scent of grass and flowering shrubs mingled with the heady scent of the flowering frangipani trees.

At the side entrance they had come up to, Conrad stood by the sliding glass doors, looking down at her. Neither had spoken since they had left the beach. It was as if they had left their freedom there. Marnie found herself straining for any sounds which would indicate someone was up in the huge house. Her heart was pounding in her chest and her eyes were wide, alert.

'You look like a frightened fawn,' Conrad observed, his voice gentle and reassuring. 'There's no need to be frightened,' he continued quietly, leaning against the door frame. His white dinner jacket was draped casually across one shoulder, his white trousers hugging the tight muscles of his thighs. 'Go upstairs now,' he quietly ordered her, 'and I'll follow in a few minutes.'

He slid the doors open for her and Marnie darted inside. She looked from left to right, her eyes adjusting to the darkness of the room after the brilliance of the early morning sunshine. With her heart in her throat she raced upstairs to her bedroom, not daring to breathe until she was safely inside. After a quick shower she decided to lay down on her bed for a few minutes or until it was time to tend to Eva. When she awoke it was well past noon and Annie was setting a tray down on her bedside table.

'Mr Wright thought you might be hungry,' the young maid said, eyeing Marnie suspiciously. 'Funny you sleeping in so late,' she remarked. 'Mr Wright slept in as well. He's only just got up himself!'

Marnie struggled into a sitting position, suppressing a smile. It made her feel happy that Conrad had gone to bed just as she had. And if Annie was suspicious, so what? She had nothing concrete to base her suspicions on and it was obvious by her prying that no one had seen them come home this morning. If anyone had, Annie and Flora would have been the first to know.

'What's for breakfast, Annie?' she asked, ignoring the sly comments. 'M-m-m, that looks good. Ham and eggs. Still plenty of ham left, I see.' Annie remained standing by her bed, and Marnie looked up, her expression inquisitive. 'Thanks, Annie, you may go now. I'll bring the tray down later.'

But Annie was in no rush. Her eyes strayed down to the carpet. 'Funny how there's sand on the carpet,' she remarked innocently. 'I've just done out Mr Wright's room and there was sand on his carpet as well.'

Marnie swallowed her coffee in a gulp, almost

scalding her throat. 'I should imagine you'll find plenty more sand in the rooms, Annie,' she said. 'Everyone has been down to the beach and not many of us shower before we come up.' She took another sip of coffee before adding, 'We should of course, and I'll make sure I do so in the future.'

Annie's eyes strayed over to the chair on which Marnie had placed her dress. She went over and picked it up. 'Would you like me to send this to the cleaners?' she asked, wiping tell-tale particles of sand from the hem.

'No, thank you, Annie,' Marnie replied evenly, looking the girl straight in the eye. 'I'm quite capable of looking after my own clothing. Now if you will excuse me I would like to finish my breakfast in private.'

Annie walked sullenly towards the door. 'Some people have it easy around here,' she sulked. 'You've been hired just like Flora and me but we don't get your breakfasts served to us in bed!'

After Annie had gone Marnie placed the tray on the table and swung her legs over the side of the bed, getting up and stretching. She hadn't drawn her curtains and from where she stood she could see the surf sparkling under the noon-day sun.

Memories of her lying in Conrad's arms washed over her, making every nerve in her body tingle with excitement. Neither had planned to spend the night sleeping on the beach. It had just happened, both of them content to hold the other until sleep had claimed them. Not even Annie's snide remarks could taint the exquisite beauty of their night spent together lying under the flickering stars and listening to the sound of the surf.

Marnie dressed in a royal blue frock with a white sailor's collar trimmed in red. The frock was sleeveless, simply cut and very feminine. It brought out the deep violet colour of her eyes, made all the more interesting by her honey-golden tan. Slipping into a pair of red sandals she made her way downstairs to the kitchen with her breakfast tray. The kitchen was deserted she saw with relief. She didn't want her day spoiled by any more suggestive and unkind remarks.

Eva was sitting on the back patio close to the pool, having lunch and enjoying the company of several of Conrad's friends. Marnie went up to join them and spent a pleasant hour discussing the dinner and the party of the night before. When she helped Eva upstairs for her nap, Eva asked her if she had had any luck searching for the diamond pendant in the box of discarded wrapping paper.

Marnie put her hand up to her mouth, a guilty expression in her eyes. 'I'm terribly sorry, Eva, but I haven't checked the box. I ... I'd forgotten all about the pendant,' she attempted to apologise.

'Never mind, dear, you've been busy. You can check while I'm having my nap. The more I think about it the more I suspect that's where it will be. It's so easy to pick things up by mistake when you're in a rush and things are scattered all over the place.'

Marnie went immediately to the back of the house where the box containing the wrapping paper had been placed ready to be burned. She sorted through it with her hands first but, finding nothing, tipped the box on to the concrete slab, spilling the contents and getting on to her knees to search through each crumpled ball.

So engrossed was she in her task that she failed to notice Conrad and Helena walking towards her. It wasn't until she noticed two sets of feet that she looked up, her face flushed with exertion, to stare into the bemused expression on Conrad's face.

'What on earth are you doing?' he asked, moving several pieces of paper away with the toe of his running shoe.

'I'm well, I'm . . .' she faltered badly, not knowing quite what to say. She certainly didn't wish to reveal the fact about the diamond pendant being missing in front of Helena, or before she had had a chance to thoroughly check in the lounge.

'I've heard of people saving wrapping paper from one year to the other,' Helena chimed in, 'but to actually crawl on your hands and knees to get it has got to be the pits!'

Conrad regarded Marnie shrewdly, his black eyes glittering with amusement. 'Surely that's not what you're doing?' he asked in disbelief.

But Helena had given her the excuse she had been looking for. 'Yes,' she answered, unable to look him in the eye. She had several crumpled balls on her lap and she fastened her eyes on these, her hands lightly touching them. 'They're all so pretty,' she said, knowing how ridiculous she must look, never mind sound.

'If you wanted to save the paper why didn't you do it Christmas morning?' Conrad sounded exasperated and she almost smiled at his tone because she was fast becoming exasperated herself. 'It wouldn't have been so wrinkled then,' he went on, as though speaking to a dim-witted child, much to Helena's enjoyment, as she laughed sarcastically.

Marnie felt the hairs on the back of her neck standing on end. Why did he have to badger her in front of Helena? At that instant she almost hated him. Her violet coloured eyes were stormy as she glared up at him and her cheeks were stained a deep pink.

'I didn't want all of it,' she managed through stiff lips. 'I only wanted . . .' her eyes searched for a suitable sheet, one that was far different from the others, '. . . this piece.'

She held it up to him and a knowing expression passed through his eyes. 'I see!' he nodded wisely and it was only then that Marnie realised she had chosen the wrapping paper he had used to wrap her hollyhock bubble bath in. She ignored the smug, almost triumphant look in his eyes as she slowly rose to her feet and began stuffing the rest of the paper back into the bin.

It wasn't until two days later that Conrad found out about the diamond pendant being lost and when he did find out he blamed Marnie for not telling him about it sooner.

'But I didn't think there was any point in raising the alarm until the house had been thoroughly searched,' Marnie protested reasonably. 'It could have fallen under the chair or been picked up with the wrapping paper,' she continued a trifle breathlessly, alarmed by his anger and knowing he had every right to be angry. Despite her almost constant searching she had failed to find any trace of the diamond pendant or even of the box it came in. She had even gone through the dust bags of the vacuum cleaner but all to no avail.

'Had you told me like grandmother wanted to, I might have found it! Why didn't you tell me?'

Marnie shrugged her small shoulders helplessly. They were standing around the pool where she had come for a swim and where he had caught up with her.

'Eva didn't discover that it was missing until just before Christmas dinner. She was terribly upset and I tried to calm her by saying we would probably find it in . . . in the wrapping paper or somewhere in the lounge. I wanted her to enjoy the evening. I wanted you to *both* enjoy it. And . . . and I really did think it would be found.'

'But it hasn't!'

'No,' she sighed, 'it hasn't.'

'And the other day when Helena and I came across you going through the wrapping paper that's what you were doing? Searching for the pendant?'

'Yes,' she answered simply.

He sucked in his breath. 'So you weren't after the paper I had wrapped your gift in. And here I thought you were being sentimental!'

'I ... I've kept it,' she told him in way of compensation, but this revelation only served to anger him further.

'What else could you do after that fantastic bit of acting you presented to Helena and me?' His eyes blazed down at her and for a terrible moment she thought he would strike her. She sensed the struggle within him as he fought to regain his control.

'All right,' he rasped, 'So you've done a fair amount of searching. What was to be your next step?'

'We were going to tell you,' she offered truthfully.

'When?' he barked. 'Next month? Next year?'

'When we had explored all reasonable possibilities of where it could have been lost,' Marnie answered with dignity, thinking he didn't really have to shout at her.

'Did you ever explore the reasonable possibility that it could have been stolen?' he asked in a patronising tone.

'Yes,' she answered slowly, reaching for her beach jacket to put around her shoulders. She felt strangely defenceless standing in front of him dressed only in her scant yellow bikini.

'Just ... yes?' He hooked his thumbs into the belt loops of the summer weight jeans he was wearing. 'If you thought it might have been stolen, why didn't you come to me straight away?'

'Well, we discounted that theory,' she told him wisely.

'Did you now?' he replied scornfully, glowing embers igniting in his eyes. 'You've searched everywhere but it hasn't been found. A valuable piece of jewellery disappears into thin air, but you discount the theory that it might have been stolen, even though the house was crawling with people.'

'Not people,' she was quick to point out. 'Guests! Your guests! Surely you wouldn't suspect your friends of stealing from you?'

She used this as her parting remark, unable to bear the dark censure in his eyes. Whirling on her heel she turned and fled into the house.

During the days which followed, and despite Eva's constant attempts to make her feel better, Marnie blamed herself for not letting Conrad know immediately about the missing jewellery. She should never have taken the matter into her own hands, no matter how innocent her intentions had been.

She avoided Conrad after that encounter around the pool. Or at least that's what she tried to make herself think, but she knew it was the other way around. He was deliberately and blatantly avoiding her. New Year came and went. Marnie and Eva heralded it in with a few glasses of sherry and some cheese. They talked until well after midnight, with Eva doing most of the talking and Marnie listening. In its own way it was enjoyable. It certainly was peaceful. Marnie rang her aunt at midnight and wished the family a Happy New Year. There was still no news about an alternative housekeeper for Eva, but her aunt assured her she was following up some pretty hopeful leads.

Marnie didn't know where Conrad and Helena had gone to celebrate New Year. Helena had certainly been in fine spirits the past few days, having the constant attention of Conrad catering to her every whim and fancy. It positively sickened Marnie the way Helena evoked his attention. She began to count the days when she could leave this place and all that it had taught her, for she had learned plenty. She had learned about neglect and she had learned about love. Both experiences had caused her plenty of pain. But the neglect which Eva had suffered and which she had witnessed was over. The love she had in her heart for Conrad would always be there, hurting her, torturing her, reminding her of what could have been, but wasn't. She would always remember what she had lost. For she honestly believed that for a short while anyway Conrad had been falling in love with her. But she realised now she had been wrong. Her heart which had swelled with love now felt shrivelled in her chest.

One morning shortly after the passing of the New Year Marnie stepped out of her bedroom and almost collided with Annie lugging the huge upstairs vacuum cleaner. Annie's face was flushed and cross looking and as she put her hand on Marnie's door to open it Marnie guessed why. Flora must have sent her upstairs to vacuum out the rooms.

'Don't bother with mine or Eva's,' she told the girl. 'I did ours yesterday.'

'It's Flora I take my orders from,' Annie sneered, opening the door. Marnie stared helplessly as Annie began pulling the cleaner into the room. It was hard to believe that she and Annie had got along so well on Christmas day, when even Flora had seemed almost human.

A door opened further down the hall and Conrad emerged from his bedroom. Seeing Marnie standing in front of her opened bedroom door and hearing Annie muttering angrily as she set up the vacuum cleaner, he asked the obvious.

'What's wrong? What's going on here?'

Annie spoke first. 'I've been sent up to do her room and she doesn't want me to. Says she did hers and Mrs Wright's yesterday but if I go downstairs and tell Flora that she wouldn't let me do her room then Flora will be real cross and probably box my ears or something.'

Conrad turned to Marnie, a quiet expression on his face. 'Is there any reason why you don't want Annie to do your room?' he asked.

'Or course, not,' Marnie returned, becoming agitated, 'other than the reason I've given her. It just doesn't need it. It's a waste of time.' Marnie met Conrad's eyes and shivered as ice formed around her heart. Why was he always so cold to her now, she wondered in despair? What had she done that was really so bad? She had kept some information from him, but she had explained why she had done that. Surely that one act hadn't warranted such punishment?

'Carry on,' he ordered Annie and then followed Marnie downstairs to the dining room for breakfast. He pulled out her chair for her and kissed his grandmother on her cheek before sitting down himself.

Marnie placed the book she had gone upstairs to get beside her on the table. It was a novel she was reading to Eva who derived great satisfaction out of light romantic fiction. Helena joined them just as Flora placed a platter of waffles on the table alongside a big jug of maple syrup and a bowl of whipped cream.

They were halfway through breakfast when Annie burst into the dining room, a box in her hand.

'The diamond pendant everyone's been looking for!' she squealed excitedly, holding out the box. 'Look, here, I've found it!'

Conrad stood up, his lips compressed into a thin line. 'Where did you find it?' he asked through clenched teeth.

Annie turned to Marnie. 'Why, it was in *her* room! I thought I'd do a real thorough job with the vacuuming and so I pulled the bureau away from the wall and there it was hidden against the wall where no one was sure to find it.'

Helena jumped up and put her arms around Annie,

giving the girl a hug. 'Why, thank you, Annie, you dear, dear girl. We've all been so worried thinking someone might have stolen it and obviously someone had!' Her green eyes bore into Marnie's face, which was white with shock. Conrad walked over to Annie and removed the box from her hands, flicking open the lid. Even from where Marnie sat she could see the jewels sparkling. He flipped the lid closed and black eyes joined green, two double-barrelled shot guns aiming in Marnie's direction.

Marnie stood up and faced the firing squad. Her small shoulders were held straight, her chin was lifted bravely. She looked only at Conrad.

'I did not take that pendant,' she declared simply and there was no mistaking the quiet honesty in her voice.

'Of course she didn't!' Eva's voice held anger, the first time Marnie had ever heard that emotion in Eva's voice. 'I don't know what's going on here,' Eva continued, rising shakily to her feet, 'but I won't sit around and watch an innocent young girl being victimised!' She faced her grandson. 'I never want to see that pendant again. It's been trouble from the start. Give it to Annie. She found it. Let her have it as a memento on *how* she found it!' Eva turned to Marnie, her face and voice gentle as she held out her hand and said: 'Let's go out to the garden. You can read to me there.'

Whatever happened in the dining room after that Marnie neither knew nor cared. The days slipped by and Conrad became more and more preoccupied. Several times she felt his eyes on her and she felt he needed to tell her something but whenever she looked his way she would see she had been mistaken. He wasn't looking at her after all, he was reading a book, or looking past her, or was absorbed in the carpet at his feet, a frown scarring his face. She rarely saw Helena.

One morning when Marnie went down to the kitchen, Flora and Annie weren't there. Conrad was preparing breakfast and he looked more relaxed than she could remember ever having seen him. She stayed in the kitchen for only a few minutes not understanding his sudden cheerfulness and not trusting it. She didn't ask why he was preparing breakfast instead of Flora and Annie. They just weren't speaking to each other and hadn't done since that dreadful morning in the dining room when his eyes had branded her a thief.

Conrad also prepared lunch. His cheerfulness was beginning to get on her nerves. She asked Eva where Flora and Annie were, but Eva didn't know. When Helena didn't appear for breakfast they thought she was sleeping in, the way she usually did. When she didn't appear for lunch they became suspicious. Neither asked Conrad where the three women had disappeared to because he really didn't give them a chance. He was too busy whistling and singing jaunty little tunes, which effectively destroyed any opportunity for idle conversation.

After lunch and while Eva was taking her nap, Marnie put on her bikini and grabbed her knapsack. For the past week she had done this, collecting sea shells and other bits of sea life for her science classes at school. In just two weeks she would be back teaching, and while she loved her job and her students the thought of returning to the classroom didn't hold the same challenge or excitement the way it had in the past.

She wandered aimlessly along, stopping every now and then to pick up something and put it in her knapsack. Her thoughts on these solitary excursions were always on Conrad as they were now. No one would ever know just how much it had hurt when he had looked at her with those darkly accusing eyes. If he had stabbed her heart with a knife it would have been less painful, and she might have recovered from a mere physical wound.

But not from this. She felt crippled emotionally. She wondered if she would ever have that joyous feeling of just being alive, ever again. In a way it was as if she and Eva had exchanged places. Eva had been led out to the sunlight while her own life was now closeted in gloom . . . and doom!

She bent once more and picked up a pretty shell. Ordinarily she would have delighted in it, holding it and examining it in great detail. But now it was only a shell . . . like her . . . and she reached automatically for her knapsack to place it inside.

'Here, let me help you with that,' a voice beside her said. A voice which she hardly recognised, for it had been so long since he had used those gentle tones with her.

She looked up at him, bewilderment in her haunted violet blue eyes. Eyes which held pain and torment. Eyes which had purple smudges under them. Conrad took the shell from her hand and slipped it into her knapsack. He removed the knapsack from her shoulder and slung it over his. They walked in silence, picking up shells and placing them in the knapsack quite as if this was what they usually did in the afternoons.

'Your aunt rang,' Conrad informed her casually after a while, breaking the silence. 'I told her you were down at the beach collecting sea shells. She wants you to ring her when you get the chance.'

Is that why he had come down here? Marnie wondered. To deliver a message? Surely he could have waited until she returned to the house, but then he had been acting so strangely all day that she supposed one further act out of the ordinary shouldn't be so surprising. Another thought occurred to her and she glanced at him sideways.

'How . . . did you know I was down here and . . . and that I was collecting shells?' Her voice was soft, hesitant, and when he looked down into her upturned face she saw that there was no humour there and he looked far from cheerful. Her heart wrenched painfully at the sight of the naked misery in his eyes. They had stopped walking, staring into each other's eyes and seeing their own hurt and misery reflected there.

'God, Marnie,' he groaned, 'don't you know how I feel about you?' The words were torn from his throat. 'I always know where you are and what you're doing.' He dragged a trembling hand through his hair. 'That time you went to Sydney and stayed at your aunt's for dinner I almost went out of my mind with worry. That's why I took your car keys. It was the only way I could think of to keep you here!'

Marnie tried hard to digest this but he could see she was clearly confused. He took her arm and led her to the dunes, making her sit next to him as he held her hands in his.

'I love you, Marnie,' he said quietly, simply. 'I think I've loved you since that first day when you came to my office. The way you stood up to me, challenged me . . .' He lifted her hands to his lips and kissed her palms and then each pink fingertip. 'I couldn't get you out of my mind. I found myself counting the days until you arrived at the house.'

'Why are you telling me all this now?' Marnie could barely force the words from her constricted throat. Her eyes were burning with unshed tears and her lips were trembling.

'I'm telling you this because I want you to marry me!' He dropped her hands and grabbed her shoulders. 'I couldn't tell you before because there were several things I had to clear up first but I thought . . . I *hoped* you knew how I felt about you and that you felt the same way about me.'

Marnie bowed her head and fought desperately to hold back her tears. He cupped her chin with his hand and forced her to look at him. Tears glistened like tiny jewels on the curling fringe of her lashes.

'Tears, Marnie?' he asked brokenly. 'Tears because I love you?' His voice was thick with anguish.

'You waited too long to tell me,' she said with a sob. 'I c-can't love a man who thinks I'm a t-thief!'

'But you are a thief!' he said, attempting a smile. 'You've stolen my heart!'

She wiped her tears away. 'D-Don't try to be funny,' she sniffed. 'Y-You know perfectly well what I'm talking about.'

'Yes, I do,' he answered quietly, drawing in his breath, 'just like I know you had nothing to do with putting that pendant in your room.'

'But why did you make me think that you thought I had stolen it?' She shivered at the memory of his and Helena's eyes boring into her.

'I had to do that,' he admitted hoarsely. 'Even now when I think of how you looked standing there so defenceless . . .!' His huge hands clenched into fists and there was raw hurt in his eyes. 'Soon as I found out about the pendant being lost I knew damn well that Helena was behind it. When Annie insisted on cleaning your room that morning I realised Helena was about to play her trump card. I knew that the pendant would be found in your room and sure enough it was, but I wanted to find out the whole story.'

He stood up and turned away from her, his shoulders hunched. 'You were right about Flora and Annie. They were Helena's cronies.' He swung around to face her, anger blazing in his eyes. 'Helena thought in her own twisted way that the reason I never asked her to marry me was because Eva stood in our way. It was Flora's job to get rid of my grandmother ... have her committed to a home ... out of sight, out of mind. Their plan might have worked if you hadn't come along and thrown a wrench into the works. So they decided to get rid of you and that's where the pendant came in. Helena had figured out that I had fallen in love with you but she knew me well enough to know that I couldn't possibly love a thief. She set out to discredit you in the only way she knew how.' A tender smile appeared on his face. 'But she was wrong about one thing. I would love you no matter what. I'll always love you!' He knelt down beside her and took her hands in his. 'Please, Marnie,' he begged, 'please say you will forgive me for the misery I've put you through. Please give me the chance to prove to you just how much I love you!' He placed his head in her lap and she stroked his hair, her touch loving and gentle.

'Where are they now?' she asked. 'Helena and her cronies?'

'Back in Melbourne. I drove them to the airport last night and put them on the plane. We'll never see them again.'

'Well, I hope all this has taught you a lesson,' she said primly, sounding very much like the teacher she was. 'Hard work is a good thing but like anything else it can be dangerous if taken to the extreme.' She tugged at his hair. 'If you hadn't been so involved with your work you would have realised what was going on right from the start. Poor Eva,' she sighed mournfully.

He looked up at her, black eyes gleaming. 'Something good has come out of it though. I found you! I never believed the right girl existed for me.' He shook his head in wonder that not only had he found her but she was holding his head in her lap. He didn't even mind that she every so often tugged at his hair. He knew he deserved it!

'Well, I guess I had better marry you,' she declared solemnly. 'Someone has to keep you from working so hard.' She tugged at his hair again. 'The house is so big,' she went on and he loved listening to her voice. 'I think with a dozen children or so you won't have enough time to work so hard,' she said, teasing him.

'A dozen children!' He pretended to be horrified. 'I'll have to work twice as hard!'

'Of course you will but it will be so much *easier*. Think of how much fun you'll have tying all those shoe laces and helping with all that homework. Of course that will come after you've changed nappies, but while you're doing that you can be making plans about how you'll teach them to ride the waves.'

He gathered her close in his arms. The haunted look had disappeared from her eyes and they were now glowing with the love she had felt for him for so long. She put her arms around his neck and murmured against his lips. 'I love you, my darling. I love you with all my heart!'

A fierce look came into his eyes. 'I swear I'll devote my entire life to making you happy, Marnie. From now on that will be my life's work.'

'And I will work alongside you,' she promised faithfully, 'to make you happy.' Their eyes reflected their love and held their promise. 'Let's go up and tell Eva,' Marnie said. 'She'll be so happy.'

And she was . . . when they finally returned from the beach to tell her!

Coming Next Month

2755 CINDERELLA WIFE Katherine Arthur
The idea of pretending to be the adoring wife of a powerful
fashion mogul is bizarre. The possibility of having to give
him up in a year is heartwrenching.

2756 GIRL OF MYSTERY Mons Daveson
An Australian millionaire is mystified by a secretive waif
who dashes in front of his Jaguar. She won't tell him her
address; so he feels compelled to take her home.

2757 AEGEAN ENCHANTMENT Emily Francis
A physiotherapist loves Greece! But her patient's older—
and hopelessly overbearing—brother insists she will never
understand their ways and can't belong. Which only makes
her more determined than ever to fit in.

2758 HUNGER Rowan Kirby
When a Canadian writer and his troubled daughter invade
an English bookshop owner's solitude, can she balance her
hunger for love with her fear of being hurt again?

2759 PAGAN GOLD Margaret Rome
Valley D'Oro's mining magnate accuses a visiting
Englishwoman of squandering her family's fortune to trap a
man of substance. Yet he defends his family tradition of
purchasing brides from impoverished aristocrats!

2760 SKY HIGH Nicola West
An amateur hot-air balloonist refuses to be grounded by an
unfair job interview. She knows exactly where she wants to
be: suspended somewhere between heaven and earth—in
this man's arms.

Available in April wherever paperback books are sold, or
through Harlequin Reader Service.

In the U.S.
P.O. Box 1397
Buffalo, N.Y.
14240-1397

In Canada
P.O. Box 2800, Postal Station A
5170 Yonge Street
Willowdale, Ontario M2N 6J3

You're invited to accept 4 books and a surprise gift **Free!**

Acceptance Card

Mail to: Harlequin Reader Service®

In the U.S.
901 Fuhrmann Blvd.
P.O. Box 1394
Buffalo, N.Y. 14240-1394

In Canada
P.O. Box 2800, Postal Station A
5170 Yonge Street
Willowdale, Ontario M2N 6J3

YES! Please send me 4 free Harlequin Romance® novels and my free surprise gift. Then send me 6 brand new novels every month as they come off the presses. Bill me at the low price of $1.65 each ($1.75 in Canada)—an 11% saving off the retail price. There are no shipping, handling or other hidden costs. There is no minimum number of books I must purchase. I can always return a shipment and cancel at any time. Even if I never buy another book from Harlequin, the 4 free novels and the surprise gift are mine to keep forever.

116 BPR-BPGE

_____

Name   (PLEASE PRINT)

_____

Address   Apt. No.

_____

City   State/Prov.   Zip/Postal Code

This offer is limited to one order per household and not valid to present subscribers. Price is subject to change.

ACR-SUB-1R

No one Can Resist . . .

HARLEQUIN
REGENCY ROMANCES

Regency romances take you back to a time when
men fought for their ladies' honor and passions—a
time when heroines had to choose between love and
duty . . . with love always the winner!

Enjoy these three authentic novels of love and
romance set in one of the most colorful periods of
England's history.

Lady Alicia's Secret by Rachel Cosgrove Payes

She had to keep her true identity hidden—at least until
she was convinced of his love!

Deception So Agreeable by Mary Butler

She reacted with outrage to his false proposal of
marriage, then nearly regretted her decision.

The Country Gentleman by Dinah Dean

She refused to believe the rumors about him—
certainly until they could be confirmed or denied!

WORLDWIDE LIBRARY IS YOUR TICKET TO ROMANCE, ADVENTURE AND EXCITEMENT

Experience it all in these big, bold Bestsellers— Yours exclusively from WORLDWIDE LIBRARY WHILE QUANTITIES LAST

To receive these Bestsellers, complete the order form, detach and send together with your check or money order (include 75¢ postage and handling), payable to WORLDWIDE LIBRARY, to:

In the U.S.
WORLDWIDE LIBRARY
901 Fuhrmann Blvd.
Buffalo, N.Y. 14269

In Canada
WORLDWIDE LIBRARY
P.O. Box 2800, 5170 Yonge Street
Postal Station A, Willowdale, Ontario
M2N 6J3

- -

Quant.	Title	Price
_____	**WILD CONCERTO,** Anne Mather	$2.95
_____	**A VIOLATION,** Charlotte Lamb	$3.50
_____	**SECRETS,** Sheila Holland	$3.50
_____	**SWEET MEMORIES,** LaVyrle Spencer	$3.50
_____	**FLORA,** Anne Weale	$3.50
_____	**SUMMER'S AWAKENING,** Anne Weale	$3.50
_____	**FINGER PRINTS,** Barbara Delinsky	$3.50
_____	**DREAMWEAVER,** Felicia Gallant/Rebecca Flanders	$3.50
_____	**EYE OF THE STORM,** Maura Seger	$3.50
_____	**HIDDEN IN THE FLAME,** Anne Mather	$3.50
_____	**ECHO OF THUNDER,** Maura Seger	$3.95
_____	**DREAM OF DARKNESS,** Jocelyn Haley	$3.95

YOUR ORDER TOTAL	$_____
New York and Arizona residents add appropriate sales tax	$_____
Postage and Handling	$ .75
I enclose	$_____

NAME _____

ADDRESS _____ APT.# _____

CITY _____

STATE/PROV. _____ ZIP/POSTAL CODE _____

WW-1-3

What readers say about Harlequin romance fiction...

"I absolutely adore Harlequin romances! They are fun and relaxing to read, and each book provides a wonderful escape."
—N.E.,* Pacific Palisades, California

"Harlequin is the best in romantic reading."
—K.G.,* Philadelphia, Pennsylvania

"Harlequins have been my passport to the world. I have been many places without ever leaving my doorstep."
—P.Z.,* Belvedere, Illinois

"My praise for the warmth and adventure your books bring into my life."
—D.F.,* Hicksville, New York

"A pleasant way to relax after a busy day."
—P.W.,* Rector, Arkansas

*Names available on request.

What the press says about Harlequin romance fiction...

"When it comes to romantic novels...
Harlequin is the indisputable king."
—*New York Times*

"...always with an upbeat, happy ending."
—*San Francisco Chronicle*

"Women have come to trust these
stories about contemporary people,
set in exciting foreign places."
—*Best Sellers*, New York

"The most popular reading matter of
American women today."
—*Detroit News*

"...a work of art."
—*Globe & Mail*, Toronto